THE
BASEBALL

A Brief Novel

JAMES
FLERLAGE

Published in the United States by DreamScapes Publishing Ltd., Cincinnati, Ohio.

First edition (print & ebook): November 2019

ISBN number 9780989828123 (Paperback)
ISBN number 9780989828130 (ebook)

For Samantha and Grace

One of the beautiful things about baseball is that every once in a while, you come into a situation where you want to, and where you have to, reach down and prove something.

—Nolan Ryan

CHAPTER 1

CELLAR DISCOVERY

Saturday, June 13, 2015; 11:59 a.m.

L ucy hated mice.

She found two in the back of the dark damp cellar, their long white bellies and stiff little paws face-up on the cool concrete floor. Her sky-blue eyes traced one of the mice from tail to head, where the mouth lay open as if gasping for air. Off to the side, a pile of broken red bricks had fallen from one of the cellar walls. Interwoven among them lay a milky-white snakeskin stretching four feet long. A chill ran up her back. Lucy swept the dead mice to the middle of the cellar floor, into a pile of dirt and crumbled brick she had swept earlier.

She stabbed at the snakeskin with the bristled end of the broom and took it to the pile. She tried to shake it off, but it remained stuck. Horrified at the prospect of touching it, she finally stepped on the skin to free it. With the snakeskin now in the dirt pile, she leaned the broom against the brick wall and pulled a small flashlight out of her jeans pocket. The cellar's sole source of light was a flickering forty-watt bulb, and Lucy's father had warned her to take the flashlight with her.

"The wiring is older than your grandpa," he'd said. "Better to be safe than stuck down there in the dark."

Lucy shone the light into the darkened corners. The cellar was twenty feet long and fifteen feet wide. She described the place as "creepy" and said it "smelled like sweaty gym socks." To her father, Danny, and her uncle, Dave, the cellar had been a castle dungeon, a soldier's foxhole, a pirate's cave, and a haunted house. It was also a shelter during tornado warnings, which were rare, but not unlikely, in Cincinnati. Lucy's eyes darted across a wall lined with old wooden shelves filled with canned sweet corn, heirloom tomatoes, and green beans from her grandmother's garden. Next to the vegetables sat jars of homemade plum and strawberry preserves, grape jelly, and clover honey.

As Lucy's dad and uncle grew up, the cellar lost its appeal as an adventure spot. They converted it to a storage area by covering the damp concrete with wood pallets. The pallets sat on top of stone pavers to keep them from rotting. On these pallets sat oversize grocery-store boxes, old military footlockers, and empty luggage. In mid-June, when the cellar was dry and the weather warm, the older grandkids fought over the twenty dollars that came with the one-hour job of sweeping and cleaning it. On Sunday, Lucy had beat out her thirteen-year-old cousin Connor in a game of rock, paper, scissors for the coveted chore.

There were six pallets, each holding eight to ten containers. All Lucy had to do was move the boxes and pallets and sweep up the dust. It should have been the easiest chore ever, except the cellar often held surprises. Bugs, rodents, and snakes dug, clawed, or squeezed their way through the cracks in the walls and ceiling to find a warm home during the winter months. Lucy felt lucky that the only company she had this afternoon were the dead mice and the snakeskin. With the flashlight she checked underneath the pallets and in the corners for more critters; discovering none, she flicked it off, stuck it in her back pocket, and went back to sweeping.

As she finished the last corner, she heard a knock on the metal cellar doors. She leaned her broom against the wall and headed to the foot of the steps.

"Can I come down?" called her grandfather.

"I'm done, Grandpa," Lucy yelled. "Ready for inspection."

She walked back to the corner, picked up her broom, and tidied the small pile of dirt in the center of the room. Slow footsteps echoed behind her. She finished the chore and looked up at her grandfather.

"Now that's a big a snakeskin." Her grandfather laughed. "Don't think I've ever seen one that big down here."

A former pediatric oncologist, Dr. Landon Myers had just celebrated his tenth year of semi-retirement, spending one day a week teaching medical students. He was handsome and distinguished, a next-door Sean Connery. Although his sandy-blond hair had turned white, his strong jaw and thin face had half the lines of his contemporaries. With spare time in abundance, the renowned physician devoted his life to diagnosing the ills of stuffed animals for his younger grandchildren and scheming up new ways to spend quality time with the older ones.

Lucy's dimples ran deep into her soft pale cheeks as she

brushed her blond hair out of her eyes. "Did you bring down the dustpan and a garbage bag?"

"No, sweetie. I'll take care of that later." He gave his granddaughter a hug and a kiss on the cheek, walked to the back of the cellar, looked in all the corners, and studied the stacks of boxes on the pallets. Lucy reached in her pocket for a hair tie, grabbed a handful of hair at the neck, and tied it into a tight ponytail. She watched as her grandfather inspected every box, tub, and footlocker to ensure they were stacked safely.

"The job is done," he said, smiling. "But I wouldn't have expected anything less from my favorite thirteen-year-old granddaughter."

Lucy giggled. "I'm your only granddaughter, Grandpa."

Landon raised a white eyebrow and looked over Lucy's shoulder. "What's that over there?"

He had spied something that seemed out of place and went over to the pallet to inspect it. A cardboard box was missing a corner, and he tapped at it with a bony finger. "Did you know there's a hole in this box?"

Lucy set the broom against the wall and walked over to her grandfather. "Yes, I checked to make sure there weren't any mice in there. I didn't see anything."

Landon slowly knelt and ran his wrinkled seventy-four-year-old hand over the missing corner. "The snake probably ate them before they had time to nest." He rose slowly, grimacing from arthritis in his knee. "Did you see what was in there?"

"Comic books, a hundred or so baseball cards, a jar of marbles, an old musty-smelling Cincinnati Reds dugout jacket, and this." Lucy tucked her hand into the front pocket of her gray sweatshirt and pulled out an old, discolored baseball with a faded autograph. She held it out to her grandfather. "This fell out when I stacked the box back on the pallet."

Landon stared at the baseball in Lucy's hand. The same hand she used to smack the winning serve for the junior-high volleyball championship. As he took it, his heart raced; sweat formed above his thin white eyebrows.

When his eyes blinked rapidly, Lucy leaned in closer. "Grandpa, are you all right?"

He wiped the sweat off his upper lip with the back of his hand and inhaled a deep breath. "I could use some water, sweetie. Can you help me up the stairs?"

He took hold of Lucy's arm and followed her up.

Chapter 2
Family Secret

Saturday, June 13, 2015; 12:05 p.m.

Her grandfather still holding her arm, Lucy led them into the garage, past "Reds Wall," a wall decorated with pictures and posters of the players from the Big Red Machine. Above the door to the kitchen hung a replica of the Reds' 1975 National League Champions pennant. Whether or not you loved baseball, being in the Myers family meant being a Cincinnati Reds fan. If Lucy had to rank family holidays in terms of importance, Opening Day was second only to Christmas. Every year, for forty years, Grandpa had sprung for field-level season tickets for the whole family, right behind the Reds' dugout along the first-base line.

As Lucy led him into the kitchen, her grandmother met them at the door. "Oh, Landon," she said. "Did you fall down the stairs?"

"I'm fine, Cindy," he grumbled. "I just need some water."

Lucy walked him to the breakfast nook and helped him

into one of the oak chairs. Ice clinked in a glass, and a stream of water gurgled from the refrigerator water dispenser. Landon looked over to see his wife walking toward them with a glass of water in one hand and a small pill case in the other. She handed him both.

"Should I call the doctor?" she asked.

"No need to call me. I'm sitting right here."

Cindy smiled. "Nice try."

She was a beautiful, elegant woman who followed a strict diet and exercised every day. Though seventy-five, she looked sixty, and her strawberry-blond hair brought out the sparkle in her hazel eyes. Lucy loved listening to her voice, which was as soothing as a warm fire on a cold winter's night. When her grandmother read to her little brother, Lucy often put her ear to the door to indulge in the butter-smooth voice that had read her the same stories years earlier. But now there was a cloud of worry over the woman she loved, respected, and admired.

"Landon, what happened?"

Lucy looked at her grandfather. She searched the expression on both their faces and was relieved when her grandfather spoke.

"Lucy found Alex's baseball."

Cindy sat in the dining chair next to her husband and reached out for his hand.

With his free hand, Landon pulled the yellowed ball from his pocket. The stitching had faded from deep red to light maroon, and the Major League Baseball logo had nearly faded away. A dark scribble resembled an illegible autograph. Landon set the ball on the table and wiped a tear from his eye. Cindy scooted closer and put an arm around him.

Lucy was confused. *Who's Alex?* she wondered.

Cindy looked over at her and smiled. "Has your dad ever mentioned Alex?"

Lucy shook her head. "No."

Landon wiped his eyes once more and twirled the baseball in circles on the table. "Please call your dad. When he answers, hand me the phone."

Lucy punched in the numbers on her cell phone. Her dad answered after the first ring.

"Hey, kid, you okay?" her father asked.

"Yeah. I'm still at the house. Grandpa wants to talk to you."

"Put him on."

Lucy handed the phone to her grandfather. "Hello, Danny? Yes, we're all fine. Lucy did a great job on the cellar. You need to ask her about the snakeskin." Landon paused for a reaction then laughed. "Yes, I think it did, but I'll let her tell you about it. Say, I need to ask your permission on something. Alex's baseball fell out of one of the boxes while Lucy was cleaning. If you don't mind, I'd like to share the story with her."

Lucy's heart pounded.

"I agree, she's old enough, but I wanted your permission first. Look, it's about noon now. How about we feed her lunch and you can pick her up around two?"

Landon kept twirling the ball on the table. Lucy was grateful his tears were gone and his deep voice and steady gaze had returned.

"You might want to talk more about it too," Landon said into the phone. "The grandkids were bound to learn all this sooner or later. I'll call David and have him send Connor over later today or tomorrow. That way they'll both know."

Lucy watched as her grandmother moved her hand to Landon's arm. She winked at Lucy as if to say, "It's all right," while her fingers lightly caressed her husband's skin.

Lucy would have given anything to know what her father and grandfather were discussing. She smiled at her grandmother and waited impatiently for the call to end.

"Thanks, Danny," Landon said. "We'll see you around two."

He handed the phone back to his granddaughter. Cindy turned to her husband. "What did Dan say?"

Landon picked up the baseball, palmed it, then set it back down. "He said I could tell Lucy the story. All of it."

Cindy patted her husband's shoulder. "I'll start lunch." She looked at her granddaughter. "Honey, if you have plans this afternoon, you'd better change them."

Lucy shook her head. "Just some studying, but that can wait."

Cindy nodded. "Good. Because your grandfather is going to tell you a special story."

"Is it a secret?" Lucy asked.

"Not exactly. At least not on purpose," said Landon. "Your mom and dad, and Uncle Dave and Aunt Linda, wanted to wait until you and your cousins were old enough. It's one of those stories Grandma and I have kept down in the cellar, along with this baseball."

"So they're the only ones in our family who know about this story?" Lucy asked.

Landon took a sip of water and nodded.

"Will I be the first grandkid to hear it?" Lucy asked.

"Yes. Are you okay if I ask you to keep this to yourself?"

"You can trust me, Grandpa."

"Good, because I want to tell your cousin, Connor, the same way I'm telling you. I'll tell the younger kids when they're your age." Landon shifted in his chair and cleared his throat. "I wasn't prepared for when this day would come."

"You knew it was coming," Cindy called from the kitchen. "The Good Lord will be knocking at both of our doors soon. It's time for the grandkids to know." She walked to the table with three empty glasses and a pitcher of tea. "Pour your tea while I make sandwiches."

Lucy poured her grandfather a glass of tea. He took a long drink then licked the foam from his upper lip.

She eyed the ball on the table. She picked it up, studied the faded autograph, and ran her thumb over the worn leather and stitching. *What kind of secret has our family been keeping?* Lucy gazed intensely at the object in her hand, looked at Landon, and spoke in a quiet voice.

"Grandpa, tell me about the baseball."

CHAPTER 3

SECOND OPINION

Friday, June 6, 1975; 9:53 a.m.

In five minutes, the dark-brown leather chairs that sat on the other side of Landon's desk would be occupied by Mr. and Mrs. Caldwell. Two days prior, the forty-something couple's twelve-year-old son, Ronald, had been admitted to the hospital with a fever. The boy had lost several pounds in a matter of weeks and complained of intense headaches, vomiting, and tiredness. The couple thought it was a virus. When the initial test results came back, the admitting physician suspected something worse. So he referred the patient to a pediatric hematologist, who ordered more blood work and a bone-marrow biopsy. When the test results confirmed the boy had acute lymphoblastic leukemia, the hematologist referred Ronald and his parents to Dr. Landon Myers, a pediatric oncologist.

Landon always pushed his pathology colleagues hard. None of them had ever personally suffered the torture of waiting for test results. Landon received the results earlier in the morning and sat down to review them. He phoned the pathologist who had filed the test results, scribbled some notes, reorganized the chart, and closed the file. Behind him on his credenza sat a coffeemaker with a fresh pot. He poured himself a cup, set out two extras, and placed two coasters on the cherry-stained coffee table between the chairs.

He then headed to the back corner of his office. A large three-foot-by-five-foot portrait of his family still hung on the wall. Parents of his patients often commented on the beautiful family and their handsome teenaged son, Alex. Landon always smiled and replied to the comments with gratitude. He never corrected people's perception of his happy American family.

I hope your marriage outlives mine, he thought.

Standing in front of the hall tree, he took off his white hospital coat, his sport coat, and finally his tie. He ignored the studies on doctor-patient transference and the time-honored traditions of delivering the cold, clinical message that focused on symptoms, treatment, and prognosis. Landon believed in having an honest relationship with the parents of his patients, even if it meant internalizing his own pain and suffering.

Although he sensed his patients' parents thought he held all the answers, he knew he wasn't a genie, a crystal ball, or a god. He was a doctor who relied on science, and science had its limits. There was always more to study and learn, more theories to test, more clinical trials to oversee, and more children coming to the hospital with malignancies. Some of them were cured; others weren't. He struggled to help each patient's parents cope and often argued with God about why children had to suffer.

Landon paused in front of the picture of his family. He was dressed in a dark suit, with a vest and a tie. Marilyn wore a beautiful black dress that accented her brunette hair and petite figure. Alex wore an outfit that matched Landon's. In his eyes, Landon observed a fiery excitement for life and a naïve expectation that things would never change. His father was a brilliant doctor, yes, with a superior bedside manner and a knack for helping kids, but what Alex didn't know was that Landon couldn't keep things together for his own family. His own kid. His own wife. The ex-wife. The woman who had left him for a wealthy business executive a month after the portrait had been delivered to his office.

Landon dismissed these thoughts. He needed to concentrate on his patient, Ronald. His parents would be inconsolable at first, but over time they could rediscover hope. He walked to his desk, opened the lower left-hand drawer, took out some pamphlets on support groups, and stuffed them in Ronald's chart. Although he had prepared for hundreds of these kinds of conversations over the years, each one had been different. He constantly reminded himself that these parents were hearing their child's diagnosis for the first time and told himself not to talk too fast or clinically. Some of the conversations went precisely as planned; others didn't. Landon reached for a box of tissues on his credenza and placed them between the coasters on the coffee table. He blew on his coffee to cool it, took a sip, and waited.

Mr. and Mrs. Caldwell arrived five minutes late. A short, wiry man with soft-looking hands introduced himself as Dennis. The wife introduced herself as Peggy. Her white hat matched her gloves, and she looked more like June Cleaver than a fashionable woman from the 1970s. After a moment of pleasantries, the couple sat down.

"Thank you for meeting me this morning. May I offer you some coffee?"

Both declined. Dennis cleared his throat. Peggy turned her head to the side and rested her chin in her hand. Instead of taking a seat behind his desk, Landon leaned against the front of it and spoke in a firm tone.

"Let me be honest. Your son is very sick."

Peggy lifted her chin from her hand. "What's wrong with him?"

"Ronald has acute lymphoblastic leukemia. We call it A-L-L."

"What does that mean?" she interrupted.

"It means his blood is filling with a certain type of blood cell the body can't use, specifically, white blood cells."

"Dr. Myers—" Mrs. Caldwell began.

"Please, dear," Dennis said softly. "Let him finish."

Peggy sat up straight in her chair. "Very well. But please use terms I can understand."

Landon smiled and nodded once. "The body uses various types of blood cells to transport nutrients, oxygen, and germ fighters. Ronald's blood has too many germ fighters, and worse, the germ fighters don't work correctly. For some reason, the body makes too many of these bad germ-fighting cells, which crowd out the good ones. Eventually, these cells overtake the blood and the body to disrupt its normal functions."

"Do you know what caused this?" Dennis asked.

"The medical community speculates, but we really don't know," said Landon. "Radiation. X-rays. Genetics. Personally,

I think genetics plays a greater role. There's nothing you could have done to prevent this."

Landon picked up Ronald's file. He opened it, searched for the pathology results, then handed the paper to the concerned couple.

"Your son had a fever and complained of feeling tired. He also had bruises on his chest and back. The lymph nodes in his armpits were swollen, as was his spleen. These are symptoms for hundreds of different diagnoses, but your son's initial blood work indicated that something was wrong."

Landon pulled another piece of paper from his file.

"After we admitted him, the second round of blood testing revealed an extraordinarily high white blood cell count. The bone-marrow biopsy confirmed the presence of cancerous cells."

Peggy's head jerked up. Landon looked directly at her.

"The cancer is treatable. In half the cases, children will be cancer free for at least five years. About half these children relapse, but with treatment they can enter remission again."

Dennis's eyes widened, and his mouth dropped open. "You're saying our son has a fifty-fifty chance of living?"

Landon kept his response short and clinical. "The medical community gathers information on this disease from hospitals around the world. Survival rates for children at this hospital are higher, but I don't share those figures because I don't want to set the wrong expectation. I don't want to alarm either of you, but I also need to be honest."

"I want a second opinion," Peggy said.

Dennis turned and placed a hand on her arm. "Peg, I don't think Dr. Myers—"

"It's all right, Dennis. I take no offense. I'm more than

willing to refer you to another physician. In this line of work, we all hope for a different diagnostic outcome."

Peggy's voice softened. "Have any of your diagnoses been wrong, Dr. Myers?"

Landon crossed one leg in front of the other. "A few. But those situations had other mitigating factors."

The Caldwells dropped their heads and leaned back in their chairs.

Landon looked up at the clock, waited a few seconds, then asked, "Shall I refer you to another doctor?"

Dennis looked at his wife. With moist eyes and trembling hands, she shook her head.

Landon continued. "I'd like your permission to speak to Ronald. I'll ask that you be present when I talk to him, but as his physician, we need to establish our own relationship. I can explain to him what's going on inside his body, what the treatment will be, and how he'll feel. I also can give him something to look forward to, such as the end of his treatment. The last thing I ask is your permission to be completely honest with him."

As Peggy reached for a tissue, Dennis nodded slowly. Landon took the lab results from Peggy and replaced them with pamphlets.

"This support group is made up of parents with children who have or have had A-L-L. Some of these parents have grown kids in complete remission. Some don't. This is a great group, and they help provide support for each other, regardless of the outcome."

Peggy took a pamphlet and scanned it.

"When do we begin Ronald's treatments?" Dennis asked.

"Next week. When you leave today, I'll have my assistant

schedule an appointment for me to meet with Ronald on Monday. We'll discuss the treatment protocol, the schedule, and post-care."

"Ronald was our miracle," Peggy said, sniffling. "I had four miscarriages. I haven't been able to get pregnant since."

"I know this is a difficult, challenging time," said Landon. "But I promise to walk with you every step of the way. Let me introduce you to Marsha; she'll schedule your appointment."

The couple stood, and Peggy took a step toward Landon. "I'm sorry about asking for a second opinion," she said softly. "I hope I didn't offend you, Dr. Myers. You seem like a smart man."

Landon offered an outstretched hand. "I promise to do all I can to help Ronald. You have my word."

Before the Caldwells reached the door, they paused to look at the portrait of the Myers family.

"Beautiful family you have there, Doc," said Dennis.

Landon opened the door. "I'm grateful every day."

As he followed the couple out of his office, he took another glance at the portrait, ignored the churn in his stomach, and shut the door behind him.

Chapter 4

Dad's Weekend

Friday, June 6, 1975; 6:17 p.m.

From the white leather seat of his blue 1972 Chevrolet Chevelle SS convertible, Landon eyed the front door of a large, redbrick home owned by Marilyn's new husband, Mr. Michael David. The radio played B.J. Thomas's "(Hey Won't You Play) Another Somebody Done Somebody Wrong Song," over the speakers, and Landon turned it off. He popped two chalky antacids in his mouth and began to chew, the spearmint foam filling his mouth before he could swallow. *Mrs. Myers. Mrs. Landon Myers. No more "Misses." Those days are over.* He took a big gulp and turned his thoughts to the Saturdays he had spent with his father, and his deceased uncle, Walter.

When Landon was a teenager, his father, Dr. Raymond Myers, had taken him on Saturdays to visit Uncle Wally at Longview State Hospital. As his uncle paced the hallway, he shook his fists in the air, shouting, "Never trust a fella with two first names! They're bad luck! Never trust a fella with two first names! They're bad luck!"

Landon, a tall lanky kid with high cheekbones and light-blond hair, silently observed his father struggling to have a coherent conversation with his delusional brother.

"How's Hilda?" Raymond asked. His handsome smile revealed narrow cheeks, and his light-blue eyes shone in the dimly lit hallway. "Are she and the girls doing well?"

"She bought me an army helmet and combat boots," said Uncle Wally, smiling. "Gonna go kill me some Krauts and Japs!" He broke off into a run, skipping in a big circle in the hallway, mimicking a parrot. "Krauts and Japs! Krauts and Japs! Krauts and Japs! Krauts and Japs!"

After every visit, Raymond stopped at the hospital vending machines to treat Landon. "Get yourself a soda and a candy bar, son."

Landon dropped the first quarter in the soda machine and pulled out a bottle of root beer. He put the second quarter in the snack machine and pulled the knob on a milk chocolate bar.

"Don't you want something with nuts or caramel?" Raymond asked.

"Nuts? I got all the *nuts* I needed earlier," Landon grumbled.

His father grinned. "All I see are cavities, and as a cardiologist, I'd have a hard time approving this combination. But it's the least I can do for dragging you along on these visits."

"Do you miss him?" asked Landon. "You know…the way he used to be?"

His father sighed. "Yes. He's the only brother I have."

As they walked to the family car, a buttercream Nash

Ambassador, Landon conjured up enough courage to ask his next question. "Dad, what happened to Uncle Wally?"

His father stopped just behind the car and turned to him. "Your uncle was a hard worker. An accountant for Ford Motor Company. He was a loving father and a good husband. When World War II broke out, we needed men. He believed the war was just, so he enlisted. Came home a decorated soldier."

Raymond leaned against the bumper of the Ambassador and stared at the pavement.

"Wally survived some of the war's fiercest fighting. But he couldn't function when he got home. Couldn't hold down a job. Ignored his wife and kids. Started drinking. I tried asking him about the war, but he'd just break down. Six months later, Aunt Hilda called me panicking. She found Wally in the backyard in a T-shirt, army helmet, and underwear. He had dug a little foxhole with a gardening shovel and was holding a rake like a rifle. Too many bombs and bullets, I suppose."

"What did you do?" Landon asked.

"I came over, and Wally tried to shoot me with the rake. It took fifteen minutes to convince him I wasn't the enemy. When he realized I wasn't a threat, he pointed to the sky and said he'd seen enemy planes. I lifted the latch on the gate and let myself in the yard. When his episode ended, I took him to the VA hospital, and then to Longview."

Landon took a bite of the chocolate bar and chased it with a gulp of root beer. "Will he get better?"

"I don't know." His father scratched at the stubble on his cheek. "It's unlikely. That's why your mother and I paid for your aunt's nursing school. We found her a job at Christ Hospital and that small house down the street from us.

She needed to be able to support her daughters after Wally was committed."

"Will Aunt Hilda and Uncle Wally ever get back together?"

"They're still together, Landon," said Raymond. "She picks him up for car rides, dinners out, birthdays, holidays, and long weekends. Hilda will always love him. She still wears her ring and calls Wally her husband. She's still his wife." Raymond took a deep breath and exhaled. "Sometimes things just don't work out, and it's nobody's fault. You just do your best to keep going."

Landon rubbed his eyes with the heels of his hands, his father's words echoing in his mind. He had to drum up the courage to step out of the Chevelle and walk up to the door of his ex-wife's house, where his sixteen-year-old son, Alex, was waiting. He always counted down the days, hours, and minutes until their next visit. He reached in his jacket pocket for the tickets and smiled.

He walked up the red paver path to the door. A black, oversize mailbox was nailed into the house to the right of the door. The house number was in large stick-on numbers. The homeowner's name in gold letters, Michael A. David, would have glittered in the sun if weren't for the overcast sky. Landon had hoped for better weather, but who could argue with a seventy-degree day in June? He had tossed a couple umbrellas and ponchos in the Chevelle but doubted Alex would use them. His son always wanted to experience the elements as if he were a player on the field.

Landon took a deep breath, let it out, and rang the doorbell. Marilyn answered, wearing a tennis outfit. Her sleek black hair was pulled into a ponytail, her long shapely legs sticking out of a short white skirt.

Beautiful on the outside but not on the inside, Landon thought.

"Hello, Landon," she said curtly. "Alex is upstairs looking for his Reds cap."

"Are you going invite me in?" he asked.

Marilyn tapped her foot. "Michael prefers it if you stay outside. It makes him feel uncomfortable to have you in his home."

"Fine with me," Landon replied. "It makes me feel uncomfortable knowing this is the house where he snuggles with my wife of twelve years."

Marilyn rolled her eyes. "Ex-wife, Landon. Let it go."

Landon tapped on the mailbox. "The lettering for Michael's name is coming off. You might want to look at it."

Marilyn stepped out of the house and shut the door behind her. She bent over to look at the mailbox.

"It looks like the 'A' is coming off," she said, trying to smooth it back into place.

"What does the 'A' stand for anyway?" Landon asked. "Let me guess, is it…?"

Marilyn furrowed her eyebrows. "Don't go there."

Landon put a finger to his lips as if pondering a difficult problem. "I think I remember now. Does the "A" stand for… alimony? Or better yet…no alimony?"

Marilyn put her hands on her narrow hips. "Michael's middle name is Aloysius. Grow up."

Landon grinned.

Marilyn opened the door, stuck her head in and yelled, "Alex, forget your baseball cap! Make your dad buy you one at the stadium!"

She slammed the door and turned around, her arms

crossed. Landon might have taken this seriously had she not caught her ponytail in the slamming door. The screaming and cursing made him laugh.

"Here, let me help you with that," he said, reaching for the doorknob.

"You're a piece of work, Landon. Your patients might think you walk on water, but *you're* the one who's the jerk."

"You left me. You win." Disgusted, he started toward the car. He turned around when he heard the door open.

A five-foot-ten, blond-haired, blue-eyed teenager with wire-framed glasses appeared on the doorstep, a ball glove in one hand and his favorite Reds cap in the other. Wearing blue jeans, a Reds home jersey, and an official Reds dugout jacket, he jogged out to his father, who was now halfway to the car, and gave him a hug.

"Missed you," said Alex. "You got the tickets?"

Landon hugged him back. "They're in my pocket."

"Alex!" Marilyn cried. "Aren't you forgetting something?"

Alex jogged back to his mom and gave her a peck on the cheek. "See you Sunday night."

As he ran past his dad, Marilyn shouted again. "Landon!"

He walked over to her and stood in front of her with his arms crossed.

"Before you leave, there's something I need to tell you," she said softly.

"You've made a career out of berating me," he groaned. "Any chance you can take the day off?"

Her voice, both gentler and kinder now, had a pleading tone. "It's about Alex."

"I'm listening."

Marilyn swallowed. "Two days ago, he had a seizure when

he was on the patio. His eyes rolled back in his head. It lasted for several minutes. I called for an ambulance."

Landon uncrossed his arms. "I was on the floor all day. Why didn't the emergency room page me?"

Marilyn bit her lower lip. "I asked the paramedics to take us to Christ Hospital."

Landon's eyes widened. "You did what? For God's sake, Marilyn, I'm his father and a doctor!"

"I'm sorry, Landon. I just didn't want to face all our old friends."

Marilyn stared at the ground. "When Alex woke up, you weren't there. He asked me why. When I told him where we were, he shut down. We haven't spoken until today."

Landon trampled on her words. "I don't blame him," he shouted. "You've done some stupid things since the divorce, but this is unconscionable. People who know and love our family are all at Children's. I've covered your ass throughout this whole divorce. I've fallen on my sword, raised you up, said everything I needed to say to ease the relationships we had together. When this gets out—and it will—I will *not* cover for you."

Marilyn covered her mouth and nodded.

Landon kicked at the grass with his tennis shoe. "What did they tell you at the hospital?"

"That's just it—the doctors didn't do anything. I'm supposed to watch him and take him back if he has another seizure."

Marilyn crossed her arms. "There's no history of epilepsy in either of our families, Landon." Her tears began to fall. "I'm terrified."

Landon took a step forward and opened his arms. Marilyn fell into his chest.

Her voice quivered. "What's wrong with our son?"

He let Marilyn go. He didn't want the hug to linger. It had taken two years to crush all the leftover petals of his feelings. The last thing he needed was the flower to re-bloom.

"I don't know. It could be diet, stress, or some drug Alex tried with his friends. I'll call Bob Carpenter and set something up for Monday."

Marilyn nodded and sniffled. "Okay." As Landon turned to walk to the Chevelle, Marilyn grabbed him by the arm. "You'll call if something happens, right?"

"Of course. You'll be my first call. Right after I take Alex to *my* hospital." Marilyn gave him a disapproving look. Landon turned around and hollered into the breeze, "See you Sunday, Marilyn."

CHAPTER 5

STADIUM SURPRISE

Friday, June 6, 1975; 7:43 p.m.

The buttery aroma of popcorn and the sweet smells of cotton candy infused the damp air at Riverfront Stadium. Alex took a ticket from his dad, raced ahead to the stairs, and handed it to the usher for approval. He hurried down the concrete steps to an area just left of the dugout, near the coveted blue seats, and stood there with several other boys who were hoping to snag autographs. For the second year in a row, Landon had splurged on season tickets, aisle seats that sat seven rows behind the Reds' dugout. Before home games, several of the Reds' players came out of the clubhouse to talk to the kids and sign autographs. Last summer, Alex had managed to collect three: one from Tony "Big Doggie" Perez, another from Cesar Geronimo, and a third from Dave Concepcion. This season, he was determined to snag signatures from Pete Rose, Joe Morgan, and Johnny Bench. By the looks of the kids' unhappy faces, Landon surmised that the players weren't coming out before the game.

Alex turned to take his seat and bumped into his dad.

"You're going to wear this popcorn and soda if you're not careful," joked Landon.

"I didn't think there was anyone behind me," Alex replied.

"I just wanted to see if you'd score another autograph."

"Nah. They're staying dry inside the clubhouse."

An usher wiped the raindrops from their seats, and Landon tipped him. After he and Alex sat down, he handed his son a Pepsi.

Alex put a handful of popcorn in his mouth.

"You were talking to a young lady outside the gate," said Landon. "Who was she?"

Alex spoke with his mouth full. "Emma Williams. Her locker is near mine, and we had a few classes together."

"She's as tall as you are."

Alex nodded. "Did you see how long her hair is?"

"It's past her waist," remarked Landon. "I've never seen hair that long."

"She says it is a pain to wash."

Landon discovered that talking to a teenager about their love interests was like trying to sneak up on a wild animal and not scare it off.

"You've never mentioned her before."

"We don't have that much in common outside of classes," Alex explained.

"She's pretty. What's she like?"

"Smart, funny," Alex began. "She's cool. Her parents are divorced too, so it's nice to have someone else who understands that."

"How did she handle her parents' divorce?"

"It's easier for her than me." Alex paused. "Her dad is a mean drunk. She wishes her mom had left him sooner. The marriage was a train wreck."

"Sounds like it," Landon replied.

Alex took off his cap, ran his fingers through his shaggy blond hair, and put it back on. He took a drink of soda and opened a bag of peanuts.

The public address announcer called for everyone to rise for "The Star-Spangled Banner." Alex removed his hat, and Landon covered his heart. When the song ended, they sat down.

"Did you see the news about Nolan Ryan last week?" Alex asked.

"Can't say that I did."

"I've dragged you to games for two summers now, and you still don't follow baseball?"

"I'm too busy reading medical journals. Tell me about Nolan Ryan. Is he an outfielder?"

Alex groaned. "No, dad. He's a pitcher for the Angels."

"So what's the news?"

"He pitched his fourth no-hitter last Sunday. Tied Sandy Koufax for the most no-hitters in a career."

"Explain why that's cool," Landon replied.

"A no-hitter is when the other team doesn't get a recorded hit for the entire game."

Alex decided to test his father to see if he remembered anything from their previous conversations about this year's Reds lineup.

"Dad, who's your favorite Reds player?"

Landon's palms began to sweat. He had a wealth of

medical information but sometimes struggled to retain an ounce of what his son told him about the Reds or baseball.

"Let me think about it." Landon tapped his foot. "I like that guy named Catfish."

Alex looked at his dad with a scrunched-up forehead. "Catfish Hunter?"

Landon nodded. "Yeah. I just like his name."

Alex shook his head in disgust. "Dad, he doesn't even play for the Reds."

"Well, here's what I do know. I know left-handed batters hit toward right field unless they're slow on the swing, and in that case, they usually hit a foul ball or a grounder toward the shortstop."

Alex tapped his dad in the shoulder with his fist. "That's because I told you that last week."

"Hey, the good news is that I listen to you. I could be one of those dads who just acts like he's listening." Landon tilted his head. "Come to think of it, I was that dad for the first twelve years of your life."

Alex watched as the Cubs' center fielder, Rick Monday, struck out. "Stop being so hard yourself. The past two years, you've made up for it. I always look forward to spending time with you."

Landon sighed. "Yeah, well, I should have spent more time at home."

"You're saving kids' lives," Alex replied. "It's hard for Mom and me to compete with that. Hard for anyone really."

"You shouldn't have had to compete with anyone."

"Yeah, well, cancer kids need a dad too," Alex replied. "Every once in a while, Mom says something nice about your medical career."

"That's good to hear, but I'm still a screw-up."

Alex grabbed a few more kernels of popcorn. "Don't get me wrong—she hates you. She hated having to share you with every other parent and kid on the planet."

Landon set his popcorn under his seat and took a sip of soda. It was the bottom of the first inning, and the Big Red Machine was up to bat.

"Who nicknamed them the 'Big Red Machine'?" Landon asked.

"Bob Hertzel," Alex replied. "He's a sports writer for the *Cincinnati Enquirer*."

As Pete Rose approached the plate, Landon asked, "What's your favorite position in baseball?"

Alex shrugged. "I don't know if I have a favorite. I watch the pitcher, catcher, and second baseman."

Landon laughed. "Okay, choose one."

"Pitcher."

"You can tell me why in a minute," Landon said. "But first, tell me what the Cubs' pitcher is thinking."

"He's thinking, *I need my first pitch to be a strike*,'" said Alex. "Pitchers worry about getting the lead-off batter out."

"I'm going to show my ignorance again," Landon began.

Alex smirked. "You do that all the time, but go ahead."

"Tell me again what it means to bat cleanup."

"The fourth player in the lineup bats cleanup," Alex explained. "You put your three best hitters up front to get on base, and the guy batting fourth 'cleans up the bases.' They're usually power hitters, with the sole job of knocking in runs."

"That makes sense. I might actually remember that," said Landon. "Who bats cleanup for the Reds?"

"Johnny Bench. The Reds' catcher."

"Is he your favorite player?"

Alex scowled. "Dad, we've been over this. It's Joe Morgan."

Landon chuckled. "I was close."

"No, you weren't."

"Both names begin with J."

A frustrated Alex scratched his forehead. "What position does Joe Morgan play?"

Landon pursed his lips and kept watching the field, hoping he'd remember before having his son answer for him. "Wait a minute. It's coming back to me. Joe Morgan plays…"

Alex's knee bounced up and down nervously as he looked at his dad in desperation. He'd spent all last season coaching his dad on Reds players and really hoped the Harvard-educated doctor could recall something from the past two years of painstaking conversation.

"Does he play second base?" Landon answered cautiously.

Alex exhaled in an exasperated sigh of relief. "Thank God you got something right."

Landon sat up in the seat, as if proud of his accomplishment. Alex just rolled his eyes at his dad's cluelessness.

"That was more of a question than an answer, Dad."

Landon decided to change topics and throw his son a curveball.

"You wanna tell me anything else about this Emma Williams?"

Alex looked to his left and glared. "Not anything I'd want to discuss with my old man."

Landon grinned. "Do you like her?"

"Watch the game, Dad."

At that moment, a crack off Joe Morgan's bat sent a foul

ball high and over the dugout. Landon and Alex stood up with their hands in the air.

"It's coming this way!" Landon yelled.

"I know!" Alex exclaimed.

As the ball came down, dozens of hands reached up. Landon heard grunts then groans as Alex's slender fingers seemed to snatch the ball out of the air. Alex jumped up and down in excitement, high-fiving the fans around him. Landon, an astonished look on his face, watched proudly as his son smacked the hands of the strangers around them. By the time the crowd sat down, Joe Morgan was standing on first, after being walked by the pitcher.

"A foul ball and two runners on base," shouted Alex. "It doesn't get any better than this."

"How's your hand?" asked Landon. "That ball was screaming on its way down."

"Dad, I'm fine," Alex groaned. "Do you ever stop being a doctor?"

"It's what I do. How fast do you think that ball was moving when it got here?"

"A hundred miles an hour," said Alex.

Landon turned to face him. "How do you know all this useless stuff?"

Alex smiled. "I know baseball."

Landon smiled. "Which player are you watching now?"

Alex put another handful of popcorn in his mouth. "Johnny Bench"

"Why?"

Alex swallowed. "Because Johnny Bench is one of the coolest players on the field. He has a tremendous amount of responsibility. He takes signals from the manager and calls the pitches; he knows where all the runners are and which plays should be made in the infield. What people don't realize is how hard that job really is. He's battling sore knees and hips, and wrestles all that protective gear every inning. And because he bats cleanup, he's always worried about where the runners are and where he should try to hit the ball."

Landon fed off Alex's energy as he listened to him describe the intricacies of being a catcher in Major League Baseball. His son was talking to him, which was a tremendous accomplishment given the last three years of hell Alex had endured through his parents' dysfunctional relationship and divorce. Landon relished the moment, grateful for yet another day to reconnect with his son.

"Your mom mentioned you had quite the adventure this past week," said Landon.

"It was weird," Alex replied. "My friend and I were out on the back patio. We'd just finished riding our bikes. Then this dizzy, sleepy feeling came over me. I sat down on one of the lounge chairs, and I don't remember anything after that."

"Where did you wake up?" Landon asked.

"Christ Hospital. Mom didn't take me to Children's."

"She told me. How did you feel about that?"

"I yelled at her. I shouldn't have, but I did."

"I understand why you were angry," Landon replied. "I also see things from her side. Many of those emergency room nurses and docs were friends of ours during our marriage."

"She should've taken me to your hospital," insisted Alex. "The whole thing was messed up."

"I'm sorry it was a tough week for you, and I'm sorry about how your mom handled it."

Alex shrugged. "I'm okay now."

"I'm going to ask Uncle Bob to check you out on Monday."

"Why can't you do it?" Alex asked.

"Because I'm a blood doc and he's a brain doc. I want to make sure we're not missing anything. I highly doubt it's serious."

"Does Uncle Bob still keep a jar of Tootsie Roll Pops on his desk?"

Landon chuckled. "Yes."

Alex grinned. "Fine. I'll go as long as there's Tootsie Roll Pops."

CHAPTER 6

WEEKEND GOODBYE

Sunday, June 8, 1975; 7:47 p.m.

A brown carryout bag sat empty on the floor of the Chevelle. Landon cruised through the Cincinnati suburb of Hyde Park as a warm summer breeze blew through his hair. Alex stuffed an enormous last bite of cheese coney into his mouth and wiped Skyline Chili off his face with a napkin.

"Don't make a mess on my white leather seats," warned Landon.

"I won't."

"And don't talk with your mouth full."

With a mouthful of chewed up food, Alex looked over at him and opened it. "You mean like this?" he said in a muffled voice.

Landon grimaced. "That's disgusting."

Alex grinned as he finished chewing.

"Still some clouds around," Landon remarked. "But it's seventy degrees."

"Both yesterday and today were spectacular," remarked Alex. "I was a little worried during the first game. Bench's homer in the bottom of the seventh inning is the only reason the Reds beat the Cubs."

"Drove in Joe Morgan," Landon replied.

"But that second game was fantastic," Alex exclaimed. "And I caught that foul ball on Friday."

Landon laughed. "It's barely left your hands all weekend."

"It was a *great* weekend, Dad. Thank you."

"You're welcome. I'm looking forward to seeing you tomorrow."

"About that doctor's appointment," Alex began. "Can I get a doctor's note to skip my appointment with the doctor?"

Landon laughed. "No."

Alex sighed. "I still don't know why I have to do this."

"Because as your father, I know it's the right thing to do," Landon replied.

"What if *I* don't think it's the right thing to do?" Alex asked.

"Then I'll congratulate you on forming an opinion and remind you that you're still a minor under the care of your parents."

"*Divorced* parents."

Alex shifted in his seat and looked to the right at the passing houses. He stuck his right hand out to catch the air and looked above at the white clouds.

As the car rolled slowly through Hyde Park, the stereo belted out America's "Sister Golden Hair." Landon turned the radio down to ask Alex a question. "Do you get along with him?"

"Who?"

"Michael."

Alex raised both hands to feel the warm air. "He's not all bad. He's a little egotistical, but usually he leaves me alone. He's not my dad, and he doesn't try to be, if that's what you're worried about."

Landon kept his eyes on the street. "Anything else?"

"You really want to know?"

Landon shrugged. "Sure."

"He shows mom that he cares about her."

Landon pulled up to a stoplight, and the blue convertible's engine idled with a soft roar. "It was my fault, you know. The divorce."

Alex turned to face his dad. The light turned green, and Landon accelerated slowly so he could talk over the engine.

"I wasn't around. Too busy trying to save lives. I was good at medicine. Good with patients and their families. Good in a crisis. So good at the latter that I caused my own."

Alex waited several seconds then asked, "Did you cheat on Mom?"

Landon shook his head. "I missed your thirteenth birthday party. I came home that night after rounds, and you were in the basement with your friends. Your mom was sitting at the dining room table with a half-eaten chocolate sheet cake in front of her. I jokingly asked her if she would share it, and she said, 'You're ten out of twelve for missed birthdays, Landon. I want a divorce.'"

Alex gasped. "She left you over a birthday party?"

"She left me because I was an absent husband and a lousy father who prioritized his work over his family."

"But you don't do that now!" Alex exclaimed. "We see

each other and talk on the phone and do more together than we ever did."

"And the painful truth is that our relationship wouldn't be where it is today if your mother hadn't left me," Landon explained.

Alex stared out the passenger window. "We're late again. Mom's gonna be pissed."

"You're the one who had to stop for Skyline after a double-header," said Landon. "Besides, what kind of plans would she have for you on a Sunday night?"

"Absolutely nothing," Alex said. "I'll do what I always do. I'll go to my room, turn on the radio, and thumb through comic books."

"Then what's the problem?" Landon asked.

"She doesn't like me spending time with you."

Landon rolled to a stop in front of his ex-wife's house. He turned to face his son. "I want you to know something." He paused. "I still love your mother. I probably always will. The feelings she has about me, they're rooted in truth. I wasn't a good husband."

"But you're a good dad," Alex insisted.

Landon smiled. "Thanks."

Alex looked at the floorboard of the car and smashed the takeout bag with his foot.

"Does what I said make sense?" Landon asked.

Alex nodded. "But it doesn't mean I have to like it."

"Your mother and I need to work on being nicer to each other."

"*You* at least try," grumbled Alex.

"She'll come around. Don't forget to tell her your consultation with Uncle Bob is at ten thirty tomorrow morning."

"What's the appointment going to be like?" Alex asked.

Landon sipped lemonade through a straw until it gurgled, signaling it was empty. He wedged the cup between his legs.

"Bob will ask you the same stuff I ask my patients. He'll ask how you were feeling before the seizure and if you're still having headaches. He'll want to know how your vision has been since you got new glasses. If you have other symptoms, don't hold anything back."

"Will I have to have any tests?"

"Possibly a cerebral angiography."

Alex took off his Reds cap and scratched the back of his head. "What's that?"

"The doctor will insert a super-thin tube through a big artery in your leg and thread it up to a big artery in your neck. Once it's in your neck, he'll inject it with a dye and let the blood carry the dye to the brain so he can get a picture of what's going on with your vascular system."

"Vascular?" Alex asked.

"Veins and arteries," Landon explained. "Sometimes we can discover or rule out things with these special types of pictures."

"Will you do the test?"

"No. It'll be Dr. Linsby. He's the pediatric neurologist who works with Uncle Bob. A neurologist handles the tests and diagnoses. If surgery is required, Uncle Bob will get involved."

"Why would I need surgery?"

"It's unlikely," Landon replied.

"Will the test hurt?" Alex asked.

"There'll be a small incision mark in your thigh that might cause some discomfort. Some patients have a dull headache afterward. And you might feel sick to your stomach from the anesthesia."

"Will you be there tomorrow, when I see Uncle Bob?"

"Of course," said Landon.

Alex grabbed the crumpled Skyline bag off the floorboard. "I'm nervous about the appointment."

"I'd be nervous too. Just remember, I'll be there to explain things. I might not be up on the coolest comic book or know much about baseball, but I do know something about medicine."

Alex grinned. "And you're pretty good at it."

Landon grinned back and reached over to knock Alex's cap off his head. "Get out of here before I get into deeper trouble with your mother."

Alex picked the cap up off the floorboard. "Thanks again for a great weekend. I love you, Dad. See you tomorrow."

"Love you too, pal. See you tomorrow."

CHAPTER 7

QUESTIONABLE TREATMENT

Monday, June 9, 1975; 9:11 a.m.

Ronald Caldwell, wearing a green hospital gown, followed his parents into the office. A pale face contrasted against the dark-brown eyes and black hair. Noticing how unusually short and skinny he was for a thirteen-year-old, Landon immediately worried that Ronald's body wouldn't be able to meet the rigorous demands of chemotherapy. Landon walked around the desk to offer an outstretched hand.

"Good morning, young man," Landon said, smiling. "Do you go by 'Ronald,' or is there another name you prefer?"

"Ron, Ronald, or Ronnie is fine," said the boy. "I answer to all three. Most people call me Ronald."

Landon chuckled. "Very well, you can call me Doc, Landon, or Dr. Myers. I answer to those three *and* a few others."

Peggy tapped her son on the knee. "'Dr. Myers' will be just fine."

"Do you know why you're here, Ronald?" Landon asked.

"I'm sick?" he replied in a half question.

"Yes. Have your mom and dad explained your condition to you?"

The boy nodded then looked at the floor. "They said I have cancer in my blood and I might die."

Landon crossed his arms. It was an honest answer.

Dennis turned to stare out the window. "I thought it best to shoot straight with the boy."

Peggy dabbed at a tear with a white silk handkerchief and stared at the floor.

"You do have cancer in your blood," confirmed Landon, "And it has a name. It's called acute lymphoblastic leukemia. You'll hear me and the nurses refer to it as A-L-L."

"What is it doing to me, Dr. Myers?"

"That's an excellent question. Right now, your body is making too many white blood cells. They're important cells that fight off germs and diseases. Sometimes, in rare cases, the body makes too many of these cells, and they clump together and eventually attack the body."

"Am I going to die, Dr. Myers?"

Answering a child's life-or-death questions was like walking on an icy sidewalk with your hands in your pockets. Landon preferred to be direct and honest.

"Do you feel like you're going to die?" he asked. "Like physically feel it?"

Peggy and Dennis sat up in their chairs.

Ronald yawned. "I feel like something isn't right. There might be a chance."

"There is a chance," Landon replied. "A fifty-percent chance."

"Like a coin flip," Ronald concluded.

"Yes. And I'm also going to tell you there are things we can do that might increase your odds," said Landon.

"This conversation isn't giving me any comfort," Peggy stammered.

Dennis stood up and walked behind Peggy's chair to put his hands on her shoulders. Ronald looked at his trembling mother and then at Landon.

"Dr. Myers, what do I need to do to get better?"

"We need to start you on some powerful medicine. The process by which we administer the medicine and treat the side effects is called chemotherapy. Are you familiar with the word?"

"A little bit," said Ronald. "A girl in my school had had chemotherapy. Her hair fell out, but it grew back."

Landon wondered who the girl might be but refrained from asking due to confidentiality policies. He had treated almost every pediatric A-L-L patient in the city. It would be helpful if Ronald knew someone his own age who had gone through treatment. Someone who could potentially help and support him when things got tough.

"There's good news and bad news," Landon replied. "The drug prevents cells from multiplying. The good news is we can usually kill off cancer this way. The bad news is we're killing off good cells too. The chemo is poison. The medicine will make you sick to your stomach, and you'll probably throw up a lot. Your food will taste funny. You might feel cold or hot or tired, and you might just want to sleep. Doctors call these side effects. But there's also medicine we can give you to lessen the side effects."

"But without the chemotherapy, I'll die," Ronald blurted out.

"Yes," Landon answered. "Eventually you will."

Dennis cleared his throat. "Can you explain how this process works?"

Landon nodded. "The entire process typically takes two to three years."

"Three years?" Peggy exclaimed.

Landon looked at Ronald. "At first, we'll give you the chemo through an IV. If we find that the cancer cells are in your spinal fluid, we'll inject the chemo into your spine."

Ronald shuddered.

"I don't think we're going to do those injections just yet," Landon assured him. "You'll start with daily and weekly treatments. How well you tolerate the drugs will dictate the rest of your schedule."

"Drugs?" interjected Peggy. "There's more than one?"

"We use a cocktail of chemotherapy drugs in the hopes that we'll kill off all the cancerous cells," Landon explained. "We follow a regiment known as Total Therapy. It was developed by Dr. Don Pinkel at St. Jude's Hospital in Memphis."

"I read about this in the paper," Peggy said. "I thought people said he was a quack."

"My chief, Dr. Alvin Mauer, along with myself and several other colleagues, went to St. Jude's to study Dr. Pinkel's research. We not only confirmed their findings, but we're also adding to them with our own research efforts. Dr. Mauer is a strong proponent of the work Dr. Pinkel's team is doing at St. Jude's. When it comes to survival rates, they've made the most progress, and frankly, I'm seeing it work in my patients."

Landon turned to speak to Ronald. "I can help you fight this battle, son. But we will need to trust each other. You're also old enough that I can be honest about what you can expect. As I explained earlier, chemo comes with serious side effects, some of which we won't know until you begin treatment. We can alleviate some of the symptoms with other medicines, but we might struggle with what to try until you've started the process. It can be scary, but we'll do this together. You won't face this battle alone."

"When will Ronald start treatment?" Dennis asked.

"Tomorrow," replied Landon.

He handed him a small packet detailing where to go, what to bring, and what to expect. After reviewing the details with the Caldwells, he asked if they had any questions.

"I'm sorry for all the tears," said Peggy. "I'm more encouraged now than I was a few days ago."

"You don't have to apologize for how you feel," said Landon. "This is a difficult time."

"But there is hope," Dennis said reassuringly.

"There is," Landon replied, then shook hands with Peggy and Dennis. "Ronald, I'll see you tomorrow."

Ronald nodded and stood up.

"Thank you, Dr. Myers," Peggy whispered.

"You're welcome."

"You two go ahead and take the elevator to the lobby. I'd like to have a brief word with Dr. Myers," said Dennis. When his wife and son were several steps toward the elevator, he leaned in and spoke in a low voice. "These odds aren't exactly favorable, Doc. To give my son a fifty-percent chance at life doesn't sit right with me."

"It doesn't sit right with me either," Landon said. "But five years ago, the answer was five percent. Now I know this might not be reassuring, but Ronald has a better shot than my patients did a few years ago."

Dennis cleared his throat. "I'm devastated. I haven't slept in two nights."

"Don't make a statistic out of him just yet," Landon replied.

"What are you saying?"

"If I had to guess, you and your wife spent the weekend at the library researching Ronald's condition."

Dennis nodded. "We did."

"I can't tell you what to do, but I'd highly recommend you stay away from the medical journals. I appreciate the fact that you and your wife are educating yourself about your son's condition, but those journals measure life in terms of time, treatment, or probabilities. They don't account for the patient, quality of life, how unique each of us is, or how our bodies and minds respond to illnesses and treatment. Cancer is as unique to the individual as a person is to humanity. Try to focus on giving Ronald the best quality of life, rather than measure how much he has left."

Dennis stood with his hands at his side, his lower lip quivering. "He's our only child."

Landon reached out and placed a hand on the man's shoulder. "The best thing you can do is take care of yourself so you can be there for your son. Go home and get some rest. We'll see you tomorrow."

CHAPTER 8
CAUTIONARY MEASURE

Monday, June 9, 1975; 10:37 a.m.

The office of Dr. Robert Charles Carpenter was the typical clinical sort, with taupe walls, a gray steel desk and credenza, and four brown chairs to accommodate patients and their families. The drab office couldn't have been more opposite than the man himself, who served his colleagues as chief prankster and comedian. If it weren't for a thick head of bushy brown hair, a short beard, and a white clinical coat with "Dr. Bob" in blue stitching across the top left pocket, his patients might have thought he was a clown instead of a world-renowned pediatric surgical oncologist.

With his door shut and the radio playing Gordon Lightfoot's "Sundown," Bob nearly missed his secret knock. Only patients and their parents knew the secret knock, which mimicked the opening notes to the song, "Shave and a Haircut."

"Two bits!" he yelled.

Landon poked his head around the door. "I'm the scarecrow from *The Wizard of Oz*. I was wondering if you could tell me where I could find my brain."

Bob picked up the phone and pretended to scream at the switchboard operator. "Operator, get me proctology!"

"Just go in, Dad!" grumbled Alex.

Landon opened the door with his finger to his lips. "Someone's a little crabby this morning."

Alex tossed a baseball up and down as he walked in. "You guys need to get some new material."

Marilyn followed, wearing a short aqua-green dress and light-brown sandals. The sight of the dress gave Landon chills, as it reminded him of their final family vacation to Cabo.

Bob walked around his desk and gave them both hugs.

"Thank you for working Alex into your schedule this morning," said Marilyn.

Bob pointed to Landon. "He would do the same if it were one of my own."

"How are Lauren and the kids?" Marilyn asked.

"They're all fine. Lauren misses you. You should call her."

Marilyn cast a polite smile and nodded. "It's been a hectic year. Tell her I'll try to call soon."

Bob returned the smile without saying anything and looked at Alex. "What's that thing you keep spinning on your leg?"

Alex grinned. "Did Dad tell you?"

Bob chuckled. "Yes, he did. Wow! A Major League foul ball. I'm surprised you haven't locked that up in your room somewhere."

Marilyn rolled her eyes. "He slept with it under his pillow last night. He insisted on bringing it with him to the appointment."

"We had a good weekend. Didn't we, sport?" Landon asked.
Alex nodded. "The best."

Marilyn wore a scowl as she spoke. "Bob, we're very concerned about Alex. I'm sure his father informed you that he had a seizure last week."

"Yes, Marilyn, *Landon* informed me that Alex had a seizure. I called over to Christ Hospital to get Alex's chart, but it hasn't arrived yet. We can still talk about his condition."

Marilyn paused and bit at her lower lip.

Alex palmed the baseball and looked up at his dad.

"Sharp-looking glasses, Alex," Bob announced. "How long have you had them?"

Marilyn brushed Alex's hair off his forehead. "We got them several weeks ago."

Bob furrowed his brow and lowered his voice. "Marilyn, I'm treating this as a formal patient consult. I need Alex to answer my questions."

"I got them back in April, Uncle Bob," Alex replied.

"Neither of your parents has glasses," said Bob. "When did you start having vision issues?"

"It's a mild prescription," Marilyn interjected.

Bob ignored her. "When did you start having vision problems, Alex?"

"A couple of months ago, I was getting headaches and having problems seeing the blackboard," said Alex. "My teachers thought it was eyestrain and moved me to the front row. My vision and the headaches got worse a few weeks before the end of school, so Mom took me to the eye doctor. Turns out I needed glasses."

Bob opened the bottom left drawer of his desk and took out an eye chart. "Stand at the door of my office, please," he said. "Take off your glasses. Start at the top of the chart and read as many letters as you can."

Alex walked to the front of the office, turned around to face the chart, and rattled off letters. Bob stopped him after the eighth letter.

"Put on your glasses and read the smallest line of print you can."

Alex read off a row of letters that was third from the bottom.

Bob didn't say anything. He put the eye chart back in the desk drawer and closed it. Marilyn shifted in her chair. Landon looked at the floor.

"What's wrong?" asked Alex.

Bob looked over at his friend. Landon looked down then up.

"You only got three of the letters in the bottom line correct," said Landon. "The glasses should have helped you read the very last line almost perfectly."

"Is my vision getting worse?" Alex asked.

Bob shrugged. "It could be an issue with your glasses. Or it could be your vision. When your eyes were bothering you, did you take anything for the headaches?"

"Aspirin," Marilyn replied.

Bob ignored the response. "How many did you take?"

"Two to four a day," Alex replied. "The glasses have seemed to help the headaches."

"But you're still having them?" Bob asked.

Alex spun the baseball on the arm of the wooden chair and stared at the red threading.

"Alex," said Marilyn. "Answer Uncle Bob."

Alex picked up the baseball and turned it over in his hand. "Yes, I'm still having headaches."

"How bad are they?" Bob asked.

"What do you mean, how bad?" Alex replied.

"Can you rank the pain on a scale from one to ten?"

"Usually a two or three. Sometimes a five or six. When the pain gets to a seven or an eight, I take some aspirin."

"Remind me, how long ago did you have the seizure?" Bob asked.

"About a week ago," Alex replied.

"And how are you feeling now?"

"I have a headache," Alex replied. "It's just a dull ache but not throbbing."

"Where in your head does it hurt?" Bob asked.

Alex raised his left hand to the left side of his head. "On my left side and behind my eyes. It starts as a dull ache that comes and goes. Other times it throbs like waves crashing on the shore, and I have to lie down. Sometimes it doesn't hurt at all."

Bob stood up, walked in front of the desk, and leaned against it. He opened his hands as if to ask for the baseball, and Alex lightly tossed it to him.

Bob smiled. "I've never held a Major League Baseball before. This is so cool, Alex."

Alex smiled. "Yeah, I think so too."

Bob handed the ball back to him. He pulled up an extra chair and sat next to Alex. "Buddy, I have to be honest. The vision problems, headaches, and seizure have me concerned. I'm going to refer you to Dr. Linsby, a pediatric neurologist. He works with me and knows your dad. He'll want to evaluate you."

"We talked about John last night," said Landon.

"Good," Bob replied. "I'm going to suggest to him that we conduct a test called an angiography. Do you know what that is?"

Alex nodded. "Dad explained it to me last night." He turned to look at his mother. "Which is why I was late coming home."

Marilyn sat up. "Well, can someone explain to me what an angiography is?"

When Bob finished the explanation, Marilyn slumped in her chair. Alex rubbed his thumb over the leather and stitching of the ball several times, and his knee began to bounce.

Landon could tell Alex was getting anxious. "The test itself is relatively routine. You should come out of recovery just fine."

"It's not just the test, Dad—it's the result. What's it going to tell us?"

"Fair question," Bob replied. "We're looking for something abnormal with your veins and arteries that would indicate that there's something wrong."

"Like what?" Alex asked.

"In this case, we're looking for a mass," Landon replied. "When cells reproduce out of control, they form masses of cells that look like white, pink, or dark blobs. We call these masses tumors, and they can either be cancerous or noncancerous. The blobs can have their own arteries and veins. If I'm looking at a picture of an angiogram, I'll look for a ball of vessels that would indicate there's a mass in your brain."

Alex shifted in his chair. "And if there isn't a mass?"

"Then we'll be on the lookout for something else," Bob replied.

"And if there is?" Marilyn asked.

"We'll cross that bridge when we come to it…if we do," Landon said.

"Don't give me that doctor speak, Landon," Marilyn growled. "I want to know what's happening with my son."

Landon adjusted his tie and looked at Alex, who was staring at the floor. "If Dr. John and Uncle Bob think you have a tumor, then we'll need to cut it out to determine if it's cancerous."

Marilyn held her hand to her mouth. Bob leaned over and put a hand on Alex's arm. "I want you to see Dr. Linsby before you leave today," he said. "If he thinks we need to perform the angiogram, I'll ask him to schedule it for Wednesday." Is that okay with you?"

Alex gripped the baseball so tightly that Landon saw the tendons flex in his forearm. Alex looked at his mom, who wiped tears from her eyes, then up at his dad.

"I want my dad to be there."

Bob looked at Landon and smiled. "Provided your dad's schedule is open, I think Dr. Linsby could scrub him in for this procedure."

Alex leaned over to whisper to his mother. "I want Dad to be a part of this. It's what he knows. It's what he's done his whole life. I want you to let him help me."

Marilyn swallowed hard and tapped her fingers on the armrest. She closed her eyes briefly and nodded.

CHAPTER 9
CUSTODY NOTIFICATION

Tuesday, June 10, 1975; 11:23 a.m.

Nicknamed "Kojak" by his golfing buddies due to his shiny bald head, prominent nose, and thick lips, Jeff Hansen appeared ten years older than his thirty-something contemporaries. Grumbling, he thumbed through the two-page letter, his chin resting in the palm of his right hand. Dizziness gave way to sleepiness, and he struggled to keep his eyes open. Jeff sat up, took a sip of black coffee, and leaned back in his office chair. Halfway through the last paragraph, he nodded off to sleep but eventually was awakened by several hard knocks.

"Mr. Hansen," shouted a feminine voice. "Mr. Hansen."

Jeff startled in his chair, and the pages fell to the hardwood floor. He cleared his throat and grimaced.

"What is it?" he mumbled as he picked up the pages.

"Dr. Myers is here to see you," shouted the voice.

With his left hand, he wiped the sleep drool from his chin

and rubbed it on his suit pants. "Tell him I'll be out in five minutes," Jeff shouted back.

The stomach acid slowly boiled up his throat as he looked at a small black-and-white photo in a tarnished brass frame on his desk. Two high school buddies in their St. Xavier letter jackets stood with their arms around each other. At six-foot-four, Jeff towered over Landon's five-foot-ten frame. Seventeen years later, Landon had retained his boyish good looks, while Jeff had packed on forty pounds courtesy of a desk job, eating out with clients, and a distaste for exercise. Two gorgeous girls, a brunette and blonde, both from St. Ursuline High School, flanked either side. The brunette on the left standing next to Landon was his ex-wife, Marilyn. The blonde on the right standing next to Jeff was his wife, Patricia.

Jeff picked up the picture and gritted his teeth as he thought about Marilyn's cold, calculated approach to the divorce. She not only had devastated his best friend, but she also had destroyed his wife's sister-like relationship with Marilyn. Both girls had grown up together in the suburb of Fairfax, where working-class families worried about their paychecks and spent their Friday nights at football games and Sunday mornings in the hard-backed pews of St. John Vianney Catholic Church. The Myers' marriage always seemed to have problems, but none that close friends and loved ones deemed worthy of breaking up a family. Marilyn tried to sway Patricia to her side, to get her to understand the loneliness and pain she felt being married to a prominent physician. Eventually, Patricia dismissed her friend as a broken person who threw away relationships in pursuit of selfish rationalizations.

Jeff looked at the wall clock and put the picture back on his desk. He rubbed his forehead and struggled with the conversation he was about to have with his friend. The letter he received would be just as devastating to Landon as the day he was served.

Toward the end of the marriage, Landon had continued working to save the lives of leukemia-ravaged children at Children's Hospital. Meanwhile, Marilyn had secretly researched family law attorneys. During a busy lunch rush at the hospital cafeteria, Landon was served his divorce papers in a way so public that it left his reputation in disarray and his colleagues and staff in disbelief. Landon called Jeff later that day, his tearful voice pleading for help. A criminal defense attorney, Jeff wore cynicism and indifference like body armor, but the cold, calculated way in which Marilyn ended the marriage was enough to pierce it. He offered his legal services to his best friend free of charge and raced to keep Marilyn's attorneys from emotionally destroying Landon and his relationship with Alex.

Jeff stood up and tucked in his starched white shirt. He tightened the knot in his black tie and pushed it up to his collar. He then put on his gray suit coat and walked to the waiting area.

"There's old Kojak," greeted Landon. "You didn't have to get all dressed up for me."

"I never know when I'm going to meet a client in public."

Jeff smiled and offered a handshake.

"Are your clients actually allowed in public?" Landon asked.

"*You're* allowed in public," Jeff answered.

"I'm in a respectable profession," Landon replied.

"Why is it that when things are going well for folks, the lawyers are thrown over the side of the ship?"

"We know the sharks won't eat you," Landon replied. "Professional courtesy, I suppose."

Jeff heard his secretary laugh. "I like your friend," she blurted from her desk.

"Yeah, well, he's like a pimple that won't pop," Jeff replied, then motioned for Landon to leave his office. "Come on. Let's go for a walk. I'm about to wipe that smile off your face."

After a short elevator ride from the tenth floor to the lobby of the Ingalls Building, Jeff and Landon exited onto the corner of Fourth and Vine. Landon purchased two hot dogs from a vendor and handed one to Jeff.

"It's warm out," Jeff complained. "And we're in dark suits."

"We can grab a coffee somewhere that's air-conditioned," Landon suggested. "By the way, how's the new baby?"

With a mouth full of hotdog, Jeff replied, "Keeping us awake." He swallowed. "I'm averaging four hours of sleep the last seven nights."

"Hungry baby," Landon replied. "You had another boy, right?"

Jeff nodded. "Anthony Daniel Hansen. Six pounds, two-ounces."

"How many does that make now?" Landon asked.

Jeff took another bite of hot dog and held up five fingers.

Landon's jaw dropped. "Five kids? Do you know what causes that?"

Jeff grinned. "Yes, I do, and I love it."

The old friends turned the corner at Walnut Street and ducked into a small café. Both ordered black coffee.

"I have six more hours until I can go home." Jeff sighed. "Man, I need a nap."

They sat at a small round white-marble table with black,

wrought-iron bistro chairs. Jeff reached into his suitcoat pocket and slid an envelope across the table.

"I got this yesterday. That's why I asked you to come to my office."

Landon leaned over to read the return address. He pursed his lips and pushed the letter toward Jeff.

"It's from Marilyn's attorney. What does she want now?"

Jeff glared over his coffee cup. "Maybe you should read it."

Landon set down his cup and sat back in his chair. "I don't think I should. It's been two years since the divorce. I've made the alimony payments and sent my child support. What more could she want?"

"Either she wants more time with Alex, or she wants Alex to have less time with you."

"What do you mean, more time? She already has him most days of the week. We divided up the holidays, birthdays, and vacations." Landon leaned over and poked his index finger into the table. "Do you know what it's like to spend Christmas without your kids?"

"No."

"Do you know what it's like to have to wait for five days every week before you can see your kids?"

Jeff took another sip from his coffee and shook his head.

"Do you have any idea what it's like to have a judge—a complete stranger to your family and you—dictate when you can see your own child?"

Jeff shifted in his chair. "No, I don't. And I hope I never will. Look, I know you're hurt. I know you're angry. And I know none of this makes sense right now."

"What does she have to gripe about?" Landon asked.

"The letter lists several complaints regarding your

custodial visits and duties. For one, you're late on the days you're supposed to pick up Alex. Two, you drop him off late. Three, you say you're going to be at his events, and then you don't show. For example, you missed his birthday party this past spring. Marilyn believes you don't value your time with Alex, and she wants it back."

Landon threw up his hands and slapped them against his thighs. "Where does she think that first-year alimony came from? Does she think child support payments grow on trees? I see my son every weekend, and, yes, there have been a few hospital commitments that have gotten in the way. But I've missed only one event, his spring band concert, and that was due to a conference presentation which I'd already committed to before the divorce."

"And the birthday party?" Jeff asked.

Landon ran his fingers through his hair and huffed. "I couldn't see my ex-wife with another man. It was supposed to be the first joint visit. I didn't think I could handle it."

Jeff leaned forward and rubbed his hands together. He waited a moment before he spoke. "She's asking the judge to rescind two of your weekends each month."

"That's half my time with him!" Landon shouted.

Several café patrons turned around to see what was going on. Jeff scowled at them as if protecting a neighborhood kid from a bully. He then turned back to Landon.

"I think I can prevent this from happening," he said quietly. "But you need to be cool."

"Alex suffered a seizure a few days ago."

"I'm sorry, Landon. Is he going to be okay?"

"Marilyn took him to Christ, not Children's."

Jeff gasped. "She did what?"

"She said she couldn't deal with facing our old friends." Landon chewed on a thumbnail. "She's just trying to hurt me again."

"I agree," Jeff replied. "But I need you to address her concerns in a letter and let me handle the rest. Mention the hospital fiasco and all the reasons you think your custodial visits shouldn't be changed. I'm begging you not to escalate this. I'm serious, Landon. Don't say anything to Marilyn or Alex. If this gets out of hand, I can't help you. And you'll be the one who suffers."

CHAPTER 10
COURAGEOUS QUESTIONS

Saturday, June 13, 2015; 1:17 p.m.

Lucy looked down at the second half of her turkey sandwich. A deli-sliced piece of turkey and cheddar cheese wilted over the sides of the whole wheat toast. Miracle Whip oozed from the middle, and a small stack of Pringles potato chips sat untouched on the plate. A half circle of red pepper hummus remained, along with several raw baby carrots. She took two gulps of iced tea and wiped her mouth with a napkin. She picked up a carrot between two fingers and slowly rolled it in the hummus. Landon could sense the anxiety in his granddaughter's heart and a growing emotional distance between them. He let the silence linger for a minute or two, hoping she would engage with him.

"This is a lot to process," Lucy began. When she looked up at him, her grandfather's face seemed to have more wrinkles than she remembered. The skin on his forehead, all scrunched in worry, drew five distinct horizontal lines from one hairline to the other. But despite the uneasiness she felt from the conversation, she loved him even more. He was still Grandpa.

"There's much more to this story," Landon explained. "Can I finish it?"

"I'd love for you to tell me the whole thing, Grandpa."

"Anything else I can answer before I pick up where we left off?"

"Why didn't anyone tell us you were married before and had a son?" she asked.

Landon had just taken a bite of his turkey sandwich. He chewed quickly and swallowed. "There have been times when I've felt like a tourist in my own life. My original plan was very different than the life I'm living today. I had to compartmentalize my life into two existences in order to help me to heal. In some ways, I needed to put behind me everything that had happened so I could move on. Does that make sense, sweetheart?"

Lucy nodded. "It's like in volleyball when I flub a serve. I have to forget that serve happened so I can make the next serve great."

Landon smiled. "Something like that."

Lucy returned the smile, which warmed Landon's heart. He felt their connection returning.

"What did Great-Grandma and Grandpa Myers think about your divorce?" Lucy asked.

"They were staunch Roman Catholics, completely against divorce. They agonized over it for years, but what they despised more was the baby out of wedlock."

"What do you mean?"

"Marilyn got pregnant with Alex during our first year of college," Landon replied. "For the sake of both of our parents and the baby, we got married. It's just what you did back then."

"So you got married, had a baby, and went through four years of college *and* medical school?" Lucy asked.

Landon nodded. "We had a lot on our plate."

Lucy bit into a hummus-covered carrot and chomped as she spoke. "What did they say when you told them you were getting a divorce?"

"My mother cried. Dad just sat there as if he'd expected it."

Lucy picked up three chips and stuffed them in her mouth. She swallowed and drank the last of her tea. Cindy got up from the table to get the pitcher out of the refrigerator. She poured her granddaughter another glass and sat back down at the table.

"Did Alex have cancer?" Lucy asked.

Landon nodded and wiped a tear from the corner of his eye.

"How many kids' lives did you save?" Lucy asked.

Landon sat back in his chair and didn't look up. It was like asking a war veteran how many enemy soldiers he had killed.

"That's a difficult question for your grandpa to answer," Cindy replied.

Lucy looked over at her grandmother to see if she had overstepped some invisible line. She wished she could have taken the question back, but it was too late. Cindy sensed her granddaughter's embarrassment and reached out to hold her hand.

"This is what this time is for, sweetie," replied Cindy. "You ask all the questions you want. No one's going to be offended."

"I'm sorry," Lucy began. "It's just that I've always wondered how many lives Grandpa saved."

Landon picked up a couple of chips. "I spend more time thinking about how many lives were lost."

"Your grandfather was special," her grandmother replied. "He was an extraordinary physician. Still is."

Landon wagged his head and reached for a napkin. "I couldn't save all of them. I tried. With every ounce of my spirit, I tried. Fighting leukemia back then was like trying to hit a baseball three hundred yards with a sand wedge. Until Total Therapy was introduced, it was a constant struggle."

"You helped some," said Cindy. "It might not have been all curative, but you certainly made an impact. And to answer your question, Lucy, the answer is hundreds. Hundreds of lives."

"Longevity stats don't measure the quality of life," Landon said. "Some of those kids needed palliative care and nothing more. But their parents –God bless them– wanted their child to get treatment. We were helping them live to reach goals like birthdays, graduations, and holidays."

Lucy took a bite of her sandwich. "Who was Uncle Bob?" she mumbled through the mouthful.

Cindy burst out laughing. Landon rested his forehead on his hand and grinned as if someone had told a dirty joke in front of a nun.

"We absolutely loved Bob and Jenny Carpenter," said Cindy. "They were our best friends from the time we got married."

"Bob was a hoot," Landon remarked. "He could tell jokes and stories that would leave you in tears, laughing. He and his wife became friends with Marilyn and me. Jenny was the one who first suggested to Marilyn that she leave me for someone else."

"That's an awful lot of dirt, Landon," Cindy scolded. "And not particularly relevant to the story you're telling."

"It's all right, Grandma," Lucy replied. "I watch *Grey's Anatomy*, and those doctors have some serious drama going on."

Cindy laughed as Landon continued. "Bob dealt with mostly terminal cases," he explained. "It always seemed he was giving bad news to his patients and their families. He taught me that transference, which is when a patient and a doctor move from a clinical relationship to something more, is inevitable when you're working with kids and their parents. He would say things like 'Don't be a robot,' and 'Love the patient, not the specialty,' and 'Empower the child.' He was a great doc." Landon paused for a moment. "I sure miss him."

Lucy wiped up the last streaks of hummus with her chips. "What happened to him?"

"He died of a heart attack several years ago," Cindy replied, then sighed. "We're still in touch with Jenny, but she's suffering from Alzheimer's and the visits are getting shorter."

"I have another question," Lucy announced.

"Go for it," Landon replied.

"When did you and Grandma meet?"

"It was scandalous," Cindy teased. "Your grandpa was a hunk."

"Grandma," Lucy groaned. "Stop it. I'm going to barf up my lunch."

Cindy laughed, got up from the table, walked to the floor-to-ceiling pantry, and pulled out a package of Double-Stuff Oreos.

"Those are my favorite!" Lucy exclaimed.

Cindy smiled. "You want milk?"

Lucy nodded and rubbed her hands together in delight. "Okay, Grandpa. The story is that you met Grandma at Reds game."

Landon grinned. "That's not exactly true."

"C'mon, Grandpa! Spill it."

Landon leaned over the table and placed his hand on Lucy's.

"Sweetie, I was just getting to that."

CHAPTER 11
CHANCE MEETING

Wednesday, June 11, 1975; 10:47 a.m.

A grunt and a gurgle woke Alex from a light sleep. He opened his eyes and looked to his left, past the chrome bed railing, in the direction of the sound. A young nurse with strawberry-blond hair held a small kidney-shaped bowl under the chin of a vomiting patient. Alex closed his eyes and looked the other way, wishing he had the strength to cover his ears. Drifting in and out of sleep as the anesthesia wore off, he listened to the retching and groaning of the suffering kid next to him.

Alex heard the nurse say, "You have the dry heaves, Ronald. I'll ask the doctor to prescribe some medicine to help with nausea. I'm leaving you with two empty containers if you need to throw up."

He watched the nurse adjust her cap as she walked away. He turned his head once more and saw the boy staring at him.

"I'm sorry to wake you," the boy said in a raspy voice. "First round of chemo. My stomach hurts, and I feel horrible."

Alex lied to make the boy feel better. "I didn't hear much of anything. I'm coming out of anesthesia; I can't seem to stay awake."

"My name's Ronald. Ronald Caldwell."

Alex closed his eyes. "I'm Alex."

Ronald sat up and reached for one of the containers. He felt his stomach contract, but nothing came up. He set it on his hospital tray and lay down.

"Why are you in recovery?"

Alex coughed and closed his eyes. "I had a brain angiogram."

"What for?" Ronald asked.

"My doctor thinks it might be cancer," Alex replied.

"I haven't met anyone here who's been through this. It would be nice to meet another kid who's gone through this chemo crap."

"I've never been through chemo." Alex shifted under the sheets and pulled them closer to his chin. "Who's your doctor?"

"Dr. Myers," Ronald replied. "I like him. He gets me. He calms down my parents. He's the one who wanted me to try this chemo cocktail that's making me so sick."

"Any chemo drug will make you sick," said Alex. "It's a controlled poison. If you can get through the treatment, you'll probably make it."

Ronald squinted his eyes at Alex. "How do *you* know I'll make it?"

"Because your doctor is my dad."

Ronald appeared totally confused, as indicated by the lines on his forehead. "Dr. Myers is your dad?"

Alex nodded.

"Explain to me again why you're here," said Ronald.

Another wave of sleepiness washed over Alex. He yawned and shifted again to try to get comfortable. "Vision problems, headaches, tired all the time. I had a seizure a week ago. My dad's best friend here is a brain surgeon. Dad brought me to see him yesterday, and he referred me to a neurologist, who decided he needed to take pictures of my brain this morning."

"What did they do?" Ronald asked.

"Put me to sleep. Stuck a big a needle in my thigh, ran a miniature tube up to my neck, and injected dye through the tube and into my bloodstream. The dye creates a picture of my brain."

"What are they looking for?"

Alex looked up the ceiling. "Cancer."

"Like brain cancer?"

"Yeah. Like brain cancer."

Ronald quickly reached for the container on his hospital tray and proceeded to fill it with vomit.

"Didn't like my answer, huh?" said Alex. He tried to offer a smile but couldn't muster it.

Ronald wiped his mouth and chin with a cloth and took a sip of water. "The stomach acid burns my throat," he said in a hoarse voice.

"That's not the worst of it," Alex replied. "Your food's going to have a metallic taste to it. You'll be awake one minute and sound asleep the next. You'll feel like you're burning up and start shedding clothes, only to pile on blankets because you'll feel like you're freezing to death."

"Yeah, that's what I've heard."

"My Dad talks about work all the time."

"What does he think is wrong with you?"

"He won't say."

"Do you think you're sick?"

"I think I'm really sick," Alex replied.

"Why do you say that?"

"I know something's not right. I've been hiding symptoms from my mom and dad. The headaches are bad. It feels like someone is sticking a knife in my head and beating on it with a pipe at the same time."

"Are you scared?" Ronald asked.

"Yeah. It's weird because I feel like I already know what the outcome will be and I'm just playing along. My parents got divorced two years ago, and I figured out that the path of least resistance is a path to peace."

"But your dad's a doctor," Ronald protested. "There's got to be something he can do."

"I'm pretty sure you're out of luck when it comes to brain cancer." Alex turned on his left side to face Ronald. "You have a better shot than I do. Just be sure to do whatever my dad tells you to do. When it comes to leukemia, he's the best doctor on the planet."

Ronald coughed. He paused for a moment as if waiting to vomit. When the feeling passed, he asked, "Do you have any brothers or sisters?"

"No," Alex replied. "You?"

"I'm an only child too. If I died, my parents will lose it."

"If my parents lose me, I know one thing's for sure."

"What's that?" Ronald asked.

"They'll stop fighting."

Ronald stared at the wall as if calculating his odds against those of the kid lying across from him. "How long do you think you have?"

"I don't know, but it can't be that long," Alex replied. "Maybe through the summer. Enough to see the Reds kick some ass this year. I think they could win the World Series."

Ronald pointed across the room. "There's your dad."

Alex looked to his right and saw the nurse walk toward them with his mom and dad. Landon's white doctor's coat swished as he walked.

"Hey, there, champ," Landon said, smiling. "How are you feeling?"

"Exhausted," Alex replied.

"I see you made a friend," said Landon. "Hi, Ronald."

"Hello, Dr. Myers."

Landon looked over and saw the half-filled vomit bowl. "Still nauseated?"

Ronald nodded. "I keep throwing up."

"I've prescribed something to help you with that."

"Dad, has Dr. Linsby looked at the brain pictures yet?" Alex asked.

"Not yet," said Landon. "It'll be tomorrow before he can get to it. In the meantime, you've been cleared to go home. Nurse Cindy will help get you checked out, and Mom's going to take you home."

Alex gestured to Ronald. "Be sure to take care of my new friend."

Landon nodded. "We will. Get some more rest, kiddo."

Alex yawned and lay back down. His mom placed a hand on his forehand and kissed his cheek. "I'll be back in thirty minutes or so," she said quietly.

Marilyn turned away and followed Landon and the nurse out of the recovery room. Alex and Ronald watched them until they went through the double doors.

"They don't get it, do they?" Ronald asked. "You know… your condition."

"Dad does," Alex replied. "He's been a doc for too long not to know."

He fluffed his pillow and turned on his left side to face the boy.

"It was nice to meet you," said Ronald. "I hope I get to see you again."

Alex mumbled as he drifted off to sleep. "I hope you do too."

CHAPTER 12
TRAGIC IRONY

Wednesday, June 11, 1975; 6:03 p.m.

Bob Carpenter slid the images from Alex's angiogram into an oversize brown folder and tossed it onto his desk. His hand trembled slightly as he reached for a plastic cup of water. He took a sip, set down the cup, and leaned back in his chair. Bob repeatedly stroked his graying brown beard, pausing once to rest his forehead on his hand before glancing at the desk clock to his right. Landon was running behind schedule, which meant Bob would be late for dinner. He phoned his wife with the news and told her why he would be delayed. She offered to postpone the family meal until he got home and encouraged him to invite Landon to dinner.

Bob had delivered tragic news for twenty years. In his third year of medical school, he discovered that he excelled at science, patient care, and treatment protocols, but most of all, at being a messenger. He had an extraordinary way of connecting with patients and their families, putting them at ease whenever he could, and remaining strong and focused when tragedy struck. But today was different. He'd never broken the news of a terminal illness to a colleague. He would go home to nine happy, healthy children. His dear friend would lose his only child, made worse by the circumstances of an ugly divorce. Bob felt like the captain of a ship sailing in unfamiliar waters.

He heard a knock on the door. "Come in," he called out.

Landon opened the door and sat down. "Sorry I'm late. I have a new patient who's maneuvering through his first round of Total Therapy. He's tolerating the chemo better than I expected, though. He's got a great attitude, and I'm hopeful it'll work for him."

"You were on the team that went to St. Jude's?" Bob asked.

Landon nodded. "It's impressive work. Hard to believe it's only been a few years since we started implementing it here."

"You're going to save a lot of kids," Bob said.

"And like you, I've lost a lot as well."

"Nixon started the war on cancer, what, four years ago?" Bob asked.

"Nineteen seventy-one," Landon replied. "Doesn't seem that long ago."

Bob patted his friend on the shoulder. "We might actually win the war on one front. Your front. A-L-L. It's becoming curable."

"I'm cautious about using the word 'cure,' but you're right. We have a shot."

Bob ran his index finger across his mustache to scratch an itch. "Alex insisted on taking that baseball with him for his angiogram."

Landon smiled. "According to his mother, he's still sleeping with it."

"The pre-op nurses had a fit—I mean, an absolute fit. I told them to put it in a sterile plastic bag and get on with it. I made sure it was with him when they wheeled him to recovery."

"It was a special weekend, Bob. I'll never forget it. We talked about deep things. Meaningful things. Things we should have been talking about for years. Girls, baseball, college, dreams. Four Reds games between Friday and Sunday."

"That's a lot of baseball for a guy who doesn't like baseball."

"I wouldn't have traded it for the world. I couldn't have asked for a better weekend."

Bob cleared his throat. "I talked to John Linsby an hour ago. I'm afraid it isn't good news."

Landon took a deep breath and let it out. "I suspected that."

Bob reached for the folder on his desk, pulled out a sheet of film, and handed it to Landon. "You can hold it up to the window if you like."

Landon took the film, walked behind Bob's desk and held it up to the office window, which overlooked the Ohio River.

"There's a vascular mass on the left side of the brain," Bob concluded.

"That's a *big* mass."

Bob nodded. "It's about the size of a fifty-cent piece."

"You think it's malignant?"

"Won't know until I get in there," Bob replied. "But likely."

Landon held the film up to the window to study it further. "It could be benign."

"It's possible," Bob replied. "But you know how this goes. With Alex's symptoms, it's unlikely."

Landon coughed and swallowed hard, then walked back to the desk and slipped the film into the folder. He sat down in the chair next to Bob and leaned back. "What do you think?"

"He'll be lucky to make it through the summer."

Landon nodded. "Thank you for giving me a heads-up on this."

Bob nodded. "You want to talk to John?"

"I'll see him on the floor later. I'll talk to him then." Landon sniffled. "I'm sorry about Marilyn's attitude yesterday."

"It's not your fault. Don't worry about it."

Landon stuttered as a tear trickled down his cheek. "She wants to limit my visitations."

"What?" Bob exclaimed.

"I talked to my attorney yesterday. Marilyn wrote a letter to the judge claiming I'm not attentive enough to Alex's needs or respectful of her schedule."

"That's just wrong," Bob replied. "From what I can see, you've made up for lost time and then some."

"Marilyn doesn't see it that way."

"You gotta fight this, Landon."

Landon sighed. "I'm running out of energy. And the more I fight, the more Marilyn wins. She seems to be winning at everything with this divorce." He stood up, walked to the window, and stared outside. "In the last year, I felt like I finally started to get him back. And now this. Not only do I feel like Marilyn is trying to take him away, but now God is."

Bob heard his friend's voice crack. He opened his mouth to say something but decided to remain silent. Landon walked back to the chair and sat down. He leaned over, put his elbows on his knees, and dropped his head in his hands. Bob patted his friend on the back, then handed him a box of tissues. Landon pulled out two and blew his nose.

"It feels like God is punishing me for screwing up my family," he said.

"I don't believe God wishes terminal illnesses on any of us," Bob replied. "This is biology run amuck. This is cells over-multiplying. This is the brain sending bad signals to the body and the body making bad cells. It's no one's fault, and you know that."

"It's a little easier when you're on the other side of the desk," said Landon. "I never thought about it happening to my own kid."

"You want me to call Father Tim?" Bob asked.

Landon lifted his head from his hands and leaned back. "I haven't stepped foot in a Catholic church since the divorce. Regardless of what anyone says, damaged goods aren't exactly welcome in the church until the annulment is final."

"If not the chaplain, then someone else. You need to talk to someone," Bob replied. "You have patients depending on you. *Families* depending on you. Most of all, your son is depending on you."

Landon reached for two more tissues. "What do you suggest we do? A biopsy? Partial resection?"

"I don't advocate either. There's research to suggest that a full resection offers the best outcome. If this tumor is a glio— and I think it is—a full resection is possible but unlikely."

Landon nodded.

Bob stood up and walked behind his desk. He took off his white coat and hung it on a brass hall tree. The green scrubs fit tightly around his paunchy middle, and he loosened the drawstring to get comfortable.

"John and I have discussed it, and we agree the pressure on his brain is causing the headaches. Alex might have more seizures down the road. We should get in there as soon as possible. Worst case, he gets some relief from the headaches. Best case, it buys you another three to six months. I'm thinking Monday morning."

Landon's eyes widened. "As in this coming Monday?"

Bob nodded. "That's my recommendation. You can take Alex to Chicago for another opinion if you want. It won't hurt my feelings."

Frowning, Landon shook his head. "You're my friend. You're also a father. You're the best in your field. Why would you even suggest that?"

"I want what's best for Alex and you," Bob replied.

Landon stood up and walked to the door. "You're his doctor. What time do you want to meet with our family tomorrow?"

"In the morning. Say nine-thirty?"

Landon nodded. "I'll clear my schedule."

Bob placed his hand on his friend's shoulder. "You know, Alex might take it better if it came from you."

"What's that?" Landon replied.

"The news. The explanations. All of it. I know you're his father, but you're also a doctor."

"I'm his father first."

"True. But Alex might want you to be his doctor tomorrow."

Landon let out a deep sigh. "I'll think about it."

"Fair enough. By the way, Jenny and I want to extend an invitation for dinner tonight."

Landon raised his hand. "Thanks for the offer, but I need to check on my patients."

"You sure you want to be alone right now?"

Landon nodded. "I'll hit the hospital cafeteria and stop by Arthur's for a drink before I head home. It'll clear my head a little."

"Don't hit it too hard," Bob warned.

"I won't," Landon assured him. "Thanks again for giving me the heads-up."

Bob gave Landon a hug. "You need anything tonight, you call me."

Landon let go, nodded, and wiped his eyes.

CHAPTER 13
CAFETERIA COMPANION

Wednesday, June 11, 1975; 7:47 p.m.

With his hands in his lab-coat pockets, Landon wandered down the corridor to the cafeteria. He heard voices talking and laughing, the clinks of forks and knives against ceramic plates, and the bell-like tones of spoons striking the sides of coffee cups and glasses. The noise seemed amplified yet muddled, as if he had cotton in both ears. Every step felt heavy, as though the soles of his brown Florsheim wingtips were sinking in mud.

He rounded the corner and entered the cafeteria as he had done every day for the past eight years. The cafeteria brimmed with nurses in white caps, doctors in white coats, and assistants and orderlies in green scrubs. With no one in line behind him, he picked up a yellow plastic tray, a fork, knife, spoon, and two napkins. He looked around for empty tables, then froze. He couldn't escape the realization that life would continue. For a moment, the lily-white normalcy of everyday monotony overpowered the black storm clouds that lurked in his mind.

"Doc Myers, what'll it be?" asked a server.

Landon turned around to see a tall, thin black man with a balding head and perfect teeth, holding a spatula.

Landon forced a smile. "Hey, Robbie. I thought you were the head chef. What are you doing up front?"

Robbie grinned. "You know me, I wear all the hats in this place."

"And the Wednesday special?" Landon asked.

"Meatloaf, real mashed potatoes—not the instant kind—and buttered corn on the cob."

"I could use some comfort food."

"This is soul food, Dr. Myers. You got an empty place in your heart, we'll fill it with good old-fashioned home cooking."

"I could definitely use some of that," Landon replied.

"We also have piping hot apple crisp with Aglamesis vanilla ice cream. Made the crisp myself, with oatmeal, flour, a little cream, and cinnamon and brown sugar. My mama's recipe."

"You'd better save me some of that, Robbie."

"I'll bring it out after you're done eating. That way the ice cream won't melt."

"Sounds good. Thank you."

Landon turned to walk toward a cashier in her midforties wearing a navy cafeteria blazer and a white name tag and sporting black bouffant hair and fire-engine-red nails. He set the tray on the counter and handed her his badge. Hospital staff ate for free at the cafeteria; it was one of the perks he enjoyed the most.

"Good evening, Dr. Myers," she said in a soft Virginian accent.

"Good evening, Gladys," Landon replied.

"You're lucky you got here when you did. We're about out of that meatloaf. And Robbie's apple crisp is selling like hotcakes."

"It smells delicious in here," said Landon.

Gladys wrote down his badge number and handed the receipt to him. "You know, I get to eat free here too. But I'm always working the supper rush, so I don't get any of the good stuff."

"Tell you what, if there isn't any apple crisp left, you can have mine. I'll ask Robbie to save it for you."

Gladys grinned. "You'd do that for me?"

"It'll be our secret," Landon whispered.

He picked up his tray and walked to the far side of the cafeteria, away from the other diners. He sat at a table for two, unfolded a napkin and placed it on his lap, picked up a fork and stuck it into the mound of mashed potatoes.

"You should have asked for the brown gravy on your potatoes," said a woman's voice.

Landon looked up to see a woman in her late twenties in a white nurse's uniform with long wavy strawberry-blonde hair, a small nose, and stunning hazel eyes. Her cheeks sunk into a pair of dimples as her soft pink lips revealed an almost perfect smile. Her plastic tray held the same special as Landon's.

Landon leaned back in his chair. "Nurse Cindy? Why are you working late?"

"Dr. Carpenter had one last case to review before he went home. I've been filing charts and films for the last hour."

Landon moistened his lips. "Did you happen to notice the patient name on the last case?"

She nodded.

"Did Bob send you down to check on me?"

"No. I just saw you over here."

Landon motioned to the chair across from him. "Please have a seat."

Cindy sat down, placed a napkin on her skirt, and removed her nurse's cap. She salted and peppered her gravy-laden mashed potatoes and scraped a pat of butter onto the gravy.

"It's a good thing you're not a nurse for a cardiologist," Landon joked.

"I used to be," Cindy teased. "But my heart just wasn't in it."

Landon rolled his eyes. "Pediatric oncology isn't exactly the first listed specialty on nursing-school forms," he said. "How did you get into it?"

"I worked for Bob…" Cindy paused and looked up. "Can I call him that in front of you?"

"I couldn't care less about protocol," Landon replied. "You can call him a jackass for all I care."

Cindy grinned and shook her head at Landon's joke. "Five years ago I worked for Bob toward the end of my pediatric nursing rotation. I graduated from nursing school a month later, and when the GPAs and testing scores were sent out, Children's called me for an interview. Bob was looking for a nurse, so I signed up. The job couldn't have come at a better time. My fiancée, Mitchell, shipped off to Vietnam about a year earlier."

Landon instinctively looked at her hands and noticed

she wasn't wearing a ring. Cindy was ready to meet his eyes when he looked up. He cut off a small piece of meatloaf with his fork.

"No ring," he said.

Cindy looked down at her left hand. "No ring. About a week after I accepted the job offer, my future mother-in-law received a visit from the Marine Corps informing her that her son had been killed in Vietnam."

Landon stopped eating and looked up. "That's awful. I'm sorry, Cindy. I didn't know."

She shrugged. "The first two years were the hardest, and the one person who helped me get through it was Bob. He found a way to make me laugh or smile every day. He and his wife took me to dinner and invited me to their house for holidays and special occasions. I've been Bob's nurse for five years now."

Landon ate slowly, stopping every now and then to take a sip of water or look at Cindy's face. She was beautiful, articulate, and intelligent and had a sense of humor. Landon and Bob had worked together for several years, and Landon was beginning to wonder if he'd spent all that time with his eyes closed. Maybe it was because he was married and divorced, and still in love with his wife. Perhaps he was too engrossed with his work to take notice of anything outside his sphere of influence. Whatever the reason, he suddenly found himself attracted to someone else for the first time in fourteen years. Landon remained fixated on Cindy's mesmerizing eyes while she talked about her grief.

"It's a process, you know. I'm finally at a place in my life where I can think of Mitch and not feel sick to my stomach or want to break down." She paused and dropped her knife and fork. "I'm so sorry, Dr. Myers. I misplaced my sensitivities. You're such an attentive listener. Please excuse me."

"It's okay," Landon reassured her. "I probably need to hear this right about now."

"I try not to read the charts as I'm filing them," Cindy replied. "Alex's was sitting there on the desk, off to the side."

Landon winced. She said Alex's name as if she'd known him his whole life.

"Yesterday, in the recovery room, he was so kind to your patient, Ronald."

"He gets that from his mother," Landon remarked. "She was the sweetest girl in school."

"Your *ex*-wife."

"Yes," Landon replied with a light chuckle. "Medical school and residency were hard on both of us. In hindsight, we shouldn't have entertained the thought of being married. Then again, I probably should have taken greater care not to get her pregnant."

"I shouldn't have gotten engaged either," said Cindy. "Mitch had a deferment for his undergrad and received another for grad school. I begged him not to enlist, but he felt it was his duty to follow in his father's footsteps and serve his country."

Landon swallowed his last bite of corn and placed the napkin on the tray, along with the utensils and an empty cup.

Cindy sighed. "I can't finish all this."

"I'm giving my dessert to Gladys," said Landon.

"Give her mine while you're at it."

"An evening walk might be nice," suggested Landon. "But I don't want to impose."

Cindy wiped her mouth and placed the napkin on the tray. "You're not imposing at all."

Landon smiled. "Great. I'll meet you downstairs, outside the lobby, in ten minutes."

CHAPTER 14

EVENING STROLL

Wednesday, June 11, 1975; 8:07 p.m.

Landon paced for a few minutes, wondering if Cindy would show up. A moment later, she rushed out of the lobby front door with her purse in hand. Her hair was combed, a slight layer of pink lipstick applied, and her perfume smelled like lilacs.

Cindy looked at Landon and smiled. "It's a beautiful night. No wind, cool air."

"And cloudy," Landon said. "Which is probably appropriate given the news I received a few hours ago."

A large crowd erupted in cheers, and Landon turned to face the sound.

"The Reds are in town," said Cindy.

"Yes, I know. Alex was begging me to take him to the game. We have season tickets down by the dugout. One of my smarter moves as a dad."

"Alex. Tell me about him."

Landon looked up at the sky. "Straight A's. Tennis player, swimmer. All-City in the three-hundred-meter high hurdles. Voted Best Supporting Actor in his last musical in a city-wide contest."

"Talented young man."

"And handsome, just like his father," Landon replied.

Cindy giggled. "If you say so."

Landon looked across the street at two boys eating Popsicles. "I wasn't there for any of it. I was always working. Somebody else's kid was always more important than my own. That's my sin."

"We all have them," Cindy replied. "Can I ask you something personal?"

Landon put his hands in his pockets. "Sure. Why not."

"I don't know how to ask this delicately."

"Just say it," said Landon.

"How are you going to deal with this? The diagnosis?"

Landon kicked a pebble into the street. "I'll deal with it when it's over. Right now I have to be strong for Alex and his mother. I've learned how to compartmentalize grief. I've been doing it for so long that it's like a second profession."

"Who will be there for *you*, when you decide to finally feel?"

"You mean when he's finally passed?"

"I didn't mean that," said Cindy.

Landon bit at his lower lip. "Friends. Colleagues. My mom. Maybe an old priest friend."

"Do you believe in God?"

"Sometimes." Landon shrugged. "In my line of work, there's a lot of reasons not to. But every year there always seems to be some miracle. Some kid, somehow or some way, seems to pull through and there's no scientific explanation to prove it. Zero."

"And you think God has something to do with that?"

"I don't know. But I do know God celebrates with those who are rejoicing and comforts those who are suffering. And I certainly don't think of God as a genie who grants prayers like wishes. I've seen families split part by some grievance, and eventually, they come together and heal. I don't know why people wait so long to make peace, particularly when it's life and death. But when they do, those are miracles to me."

Cindy moved closer to Landon. "I noticed a baseball in a plastic bag in Alex's hand. Does he play?"

"Not anymore. He lost interest as he got older. Too many splinters from riding the bench. He struggled with batting. I got him some coaching in the offseason, but he just doesn't have the knack for it."

"I love baseball," Cindy replied. "My three brothers all played. My dad's a devoted Reds fan. We should get him together with Alex. They'd have a blast."

"At least he'd get to meet someone who knows as much about baseball as he does."

"So what's the story with the baseball?"

"He caught a foul ball last weekend. It hasn't left his side since."

"That's wonderful," said Cindy. "My brothers have tried for years to catch a foul ball at Riverfront."

"Alex tried explaining the odds of catching a foul ball at a Major League game."

Cindy chuckled. "You obviously didn't play baseball growing up."

"I didn't. I swam and played tennis. My dad wasn't really into sports."

"What did he do for a living?"

Landon stopped to pick up an empty soda can that had fallen off a heap of trash. He squished the can back into the trash receptacle, and the two kept walking.

"He was a cardiologist."

"Really? Is that what made you interested in medicine?"

"Probably. I was an only child. Mom was a homemaker. Our lives revolved around his schedule, the hospital, and the country club."

"Where did you grow up?" Cindy asked.

"Mariemont. Went to an all-boys Catholic high school. What about you?"

"I grew up in Madeira. My younger sister and I attended Catholic schools too."

"Where did you go to high school?"

"Ursuline."

"That's where my ex-wife Marilyn went."

"How did you meet her?"

"We were friends in elementary school. I went to St. X, and she went to Ursuline, but we stayed in touch. She's from Fairfax, so it made dating easy."

"How do you know Bob?" Cindy asked.

"Early in my residency, I met him in the cafeteria line." Landon chuckled. "We barely knew each other, and he tried to slip a plastic cockroach in my beef stroganoff. We've been buddies ever since."

Cindy laughed. "That sounds like Bob. He's a great guy."

"One of the best I know," said Landon.

"He's so good with his patients."

"He breaks a lot of rules when it comes to patient protocol, but he breaks the right rules. I learned everything I know about patient care from him."

"I've heard you're becoming one of the best doctors in your field," Cindy said.

Landon grinned. "I don't know about that, but I'm trying."

"Do you mind if I ask you about Alex's situation?"

"Not at all."

"What are you going to tell him?"

Landon slowed his pace. "I always shoot straight with my patients. I lay down the facts, any options, and the prognosis. I'll ask him if there's anything he wants to talk about."

"It's not my place, but can I suggest something?"

"Sure."

"Tell him how important he is to you, how much you love him, and that you'll be there to walk with him through everything that happens."

They strolled for a while in silence before turning the corner.

Landon spoke softly. "That might be the most valuable advice I've heard all day."

Cindy let out a long breath.

"Will you be at our meeting tomorrow?" Landon asked.

He already knew the answer, but he wanted to gauge her reaction. Cindy raised an eyebrow. "I'll be at my desk," she said slowly. "As you know, nurses aren't usually present for patient consults."

"Do you mind being at this one?"

"I can be."

The hospital lobby was in sight. Landon slowed his pace.

"I'd like Alex to meet the nurse who'll be caring for him through this process. I also think having another woman in the room, particularly the one caring for our son, could be a comfort to Marilyn."

Cindy stopped walking and turned to face Landon. "I'd be honored to help in any way I can, Dr. Myers."

"Call me Landon, please."

She smiled, and when she did, a warm wave fell over him.

"Landon," she began, "I would be honored to help you in any way I can. But I should remind you, that in a clinical setting, I need to be in the practice of calling you Dr. Myers."

Landon grinned and looked down at the ground. "Understood," he mumbled.

Cindy reached out her hand and lifted his face. Her eyes twinkled. "I'll see you tomorrow morning, Dr. Myers."

"See you tomorrow, Nurse Cindy."

CHAPTER 15

BROKEN DREAMS

Thursday, June 12, 1975; 9:23 a.m.

Bob pulled two extra chairs into his office, set out a box of tissues, and sat behind his desk. Landon stood in the corner, holding a coffee cup in his right hand and Alex's radiology report in the other. There was a knock on the door, and Bob walked over to open it.

"Come in, Cindy. Have a seat."

"Thank you, Dr. Carpenter," she replied. She gave Landon a quick wink.

"I think it's a great idea to have you here during this consult." Bob handed her a legal pad and his fountain pen. "If you don't mind, could you take notes for us?"

"I'd be happy to," she replied.

Another knock. Bob raised his eyebrows, and Landon nodded to indicate he was ready. Alex and Marilyn walked into the office. Michael followed behind them. He stood six-foot-four, with brown hair and eyes and chubby cheeks. To

Landon, his physique reflected that of a former athlete, but his beer gut indicated that Michael had hung up his jock strap years ago. The moment Bob realized he had run out of chairs, Cindy stood and offered her seat to Michael. Bob motioned for Cindy to sit at his desk, and the awkward game of musical chairs was accompanied by pleasant greetings and introductions. Alex took the chair near his dad.

"Still carrying that baseball?" Landon asked.

Alex grinned.

"He sleeps with it," Michael said in a gruff voice.

"Catching a foul ball at Riverfront Stadium is a pretty cool thing," Bob said. "Who was batting?"

"Joe Morgan," Alex replied.

"That had to be a thrill."

Alex leaned over and scanned the desk.

"Are you looking for something?" Bob asked.

"Where are the Tootsie Roll Pops, Uncle Bob?"

"Aren't you a little old for that now?" grumbled Marilyn.

Several chuckles lightened the mood. Bob walked over to his desk and took a large candy jar out of the bottom drawer. He removed the lid and handed the jar to Alex.

"Take as many as you want."

Alex pulled out two cherry-flavored suckers and put the jar back on the desk.

"I'll leave the lid off," joked Bob.

"Michael, this is Bob Carpenter," Marilyn said. "He's an old family friend, the one we call Uncle Bob."

"I wouldn't call me 'old,' Marilyn," Bob teased. He offered a handshake to Michael and leaned against his desk. He looked down at the nervous sixteen-year-old in front of him.

"Alex, we're going to review your test results and talk

about next steps. The young lady joining us today is my nurse, Cindy Donovan. She'll be taking notes for me. I've asked your dad to go over your chart and the results with you. Are you comfortable with that?"

Alex nodded.

The office was a tight fit with all the chairs and people. Landon and Bob switched places so Landon could sit on the desk in front of his son.

"Uncle Bob, Dr. Linsby, and I have talked about the angiogram, your symptoms, and what to do next. It's not good news, pal."

Marilyn shifted in her chair. Michael reached out to hold her hand, the gesture eliciting stares from everyone in the room, including Landon. Landon cleared his throat and pulled the film from the large brown envelope. He held up the film so that the light coming through the window would illuminate it.

"This is the picture taken of the blood vessels in your brain," Landon said. "What we were looking for, and hoped not to find, was a collection of balled up vessels. Unfortunately, son, we found some." He removed a pen from his clinical coat pocket and circled an area on the film. "This area here on the left side, where your headaches are, shows an oversize collection of blood vessels."

"What does that mean?" Michael chimed in.

Landon ignored him, his eyes fixed on Alex. "Son, this indicates that you have a mass in your brain."

"Like a tumor?" Alex asked.

"Yes."

Marilyn couldn't hold in her emotions any longer. "That

can't be a tumor, Landon," she said in an exasperated voice. "He's too young."

"There's a slight chance it could be benign, Alex," Landon continued. "But the seizure, sleepiness, and headaches are serious symptoms."

"If I have cancer, what kind is it?" Alex asked.

"We think the type of tumor you have is glioma. These types of tumors are made up of cells called astrocytes, and a type of cancer known as astrocytoma. We grade the tumors by how fast they grow. Yours is sizable. Uncle Bob thinks you have a grade-four tumor, which we call glioblastoma multiforme. It's extremely rare in young people, but Bob and Dr. Linsby have seen a handful of cases."

Alex squeezed the baseball repeatedly. He looked at his mother's tear-stained face and turned back to his dad. "How did I get this?" he asked.

"There's nothing you did to get it," Landon replied. "We think it's genetic, and there's nothing anyone could have done to prevent it."

"It's serious, isn't it?"

Landon took a second to collect himself.

"Yes, son."

Michael interrupted the flow of conversation. "Marilyn, if you want a second opinion, we can get out of here now."

Bob looked Landon, who remained expressionless. Cindy shifted in her chair and kept her face down as she scribbled notes.

"He's just doing this to win his son's affection, Marilyn," continued Michael. "We need to talk to someone else."

Bob cleared his throat and gave Michael a stern look. "*Dr.*

Myers is a highly respected colleague and a trusted friend. You need to hear him out."

"You stay out of this!" Michael barked. "Marilyn, you can't expect me to believe he's not manipulating this situation to his favor."

Landon shifted against the desk. He dropped his head and crossed one leg in front of the other. He tilted his head and looked at Marilyn, who shook uncontrollably through silent sobs.

"Marilyn," said Michael. "Marilyn."

"Oh, shut up Michael!" she shouted.

She grabbed the box of tissues from Bob's desk and laid them on her lap. The ten seconds of silence that passed froze everyone in the room. Alex finally broke the silence with a question.

"Dad, am I going to die?"

Landon's lower lip quivered. "Yes."

Alex took a deep breath and exhaled. "When?" he asked softly.

"Weeks. Maybe months. We won't know until Uncle Bob removes the tumor."

"So I need surgery," Alex concluded.

"Yes."

Bob walked from behind his desk and stood next to Landon. "If I remove the tumor, it'll relieve your symptoms and buy you some time," he explained. "It won't cure you. The tumor will probably come back, and if it does, it'll come back with a vengeance."

"What if it's not cancerous?" Alex asked.

"That's better news, but there are still serious risks with the surgery. You might wake up and not be able to speak or walk. Or a blood vessel might burst and Bob won't be able to get the bleeding under control. Those aren't good outcomes, son."

"Can I avoid the surgery?" Alex asked.

"You can," Landon replied. "But the headaches will get so bad you won't be able to stand it."

"They can't be any worse than what I'm feeling now," Alex replied.

"They'll be worse," Bob echoed. "In that case, we put you on pain meds for a while until the tumor causes you to become unconscious. A vessel, or vessels, will eventually burst and the brain will shut down."

"What if the medicines don't help with the pain?" Alex asked.

Landon shifted on the desk. "We'll turn to what's called palliative care. In the absolute worst cases, we say our good-byes and put you on so much medicine that you sleep all the time and can't feel anything. Eventually, the brain stops functioning and your body shuts down."

One lonely tear streaked down Alex's cheek. He bit his lower lip. He looked at his mom and reached for her hand then looked back at Uncle Bob and his dad.

"When will I have surgery?"

Bob folded his arms. "I'd like to get you in this coming Monday. It appears to be a big tumor, Alex. It has the surface area of a fifty-cent piece. If we're going to do something, it needs to be soon."

"Do I have to do chemo?" Alex asked.

Bob stroked his beard. "There are some clinical trials available that are studying the effects of chemo on brain tumors, but none of them appear to be working. If you want to try it, it's up to you and your folks. But I can't say I'm in favor of it."

"Why's that?" Marilyn asked.

"It ruins the patient's quality of life," Bob replied. "If I were Alex, I'd rather be upright to the bitter end, rather than lying in a hospital bed."

"I really think we should discuss this," Michael whispered to Marilyn.

Marilyn blew her nose and wadded up the tissue. "Michael, I love you. I know this is hard for you to accept, and I know you're just trying to do what's best. For all his faults, Landon is the best doctor in his field and, as far as I'm concerned, on the planet. It's what he does; it's what he lives for…so much that it cost him his marriage. And this process, whatever it is or however long it takes, will hurt him the most because he, of all people, can't save our son." Marilyn wiped her eyes. "I trust their judgment, Michael. If there were anything else that could be done for Alex, these two men would be doing it right now. You need to leave this alone and just support me."

Michael, his cheeks reddened, leaned back in his chair. Marilyn turned her chair to face Alex. She took the ball from his left hand and put it on Bob's desk. She held both his hands, looked into his wet eyes, and forced a smile.

"We'll get through this. I'll be with you. More important, your dad will be with you through the entire process. You won't walk this journey alone. I promise."

Marilyn looked up at her ex-husband.

Landon wiped his eyes and said in a tender voice, "Thank you, Marilyn."

She leaned back in her chair. "Schedule the surgery, Bob."

Bob nodded and motioned to Cindy, who was facedown in her legal pad. She stood up and left the room.

Landon got down on one knee in front of Alex and Marilyn. "Is there anything else either of you wants to ask?

Marilyn looked at Alex. He lifted his head and reached for the baseball on Bob's desk.

"Can we go to the Reds game tonight?"

Soft sniffles, mixed with chuckles, filled the room.

"Sure, pal."

Alex turned to his mom. "Do you want to go with us?"

Marilyn looked at Landon as if asking permission. He nodded. She looked back at Alex and smiled. "I'd love to," she replied.

CHAPTER 16

PIERCING ARMOR

Thursday, June 12, 1975; 7:02 p.m.

Landon followed Marilyn down the concrete steps of Riverfront Stadium. She stopped suddenly, causing him to jerk the cardboard tray containing two Hudepohl beers and a Pepsi.

"Marilyn," he grunted, "you can't just stop abruptly like that on the stairs. I almost spilled this all over you."

She ignored his remark. "I still don't understand why you just didn't buy the rest of the snacks at the concession stand."

"Alex and I like to buy some of our stuff from the vendors," Landon explained. "They're on commission. They only make money if they sell something from their tubs."

Marilyn pointed to Alex. "Why is he talking to that ballplayer?"

Once again Alex had raced to the bottom of the steps near the dugout to see if any of the Reds players were out signing autographs.

Landon lowered the tray and poked his head around Marilyn. "Holy crap!" he shouted in a whisper. "That's Joe Morgan."

"Who's that?"

"The second baseman for the Reds!" Landon said. "He's the guy who hit the foul ball Alex caught!"

"The one he's been carrying around…"

"Yes! He's Alex's favorite player."

Landon and Marilyn watched as Alex handed Joe Morgan the baseball and a Sharpie.

"Oh, I wish I had my camera!" Marilyn exclaimed.

Over her shoulder, Landon watched #8 shake his son's hand and pat him on the shoulder. When Morgan stepped into the dugout, Alex turned around and held the ball high in the air to show his parents.

"Marilyn, stop waving and keep walking," Landon said. "We're holding up the show."

She hurried down the stairs and gave her son a big hug, followed by a kiss on the cheek. Alex quickly wiped the spot where her lips had touched his skin.

"Was that really necessary, Mom?"

"Oh, honey, I'm so proud of you!"

Alex furrowed his brow and spoke sarcastically. "That's something you say after I get a great report card, not for hustling autographs at a Reds game."

Marilyn hugged him once more and headed to her seat. Landon stood there holding warm beers and watery soda in the cardboard tray.

"How cool was that!" he told Alex.

"Totally," Alex replied. "I can't believe I got Joe Morgan's autograph. I told him it was his foul ball from last week."

"You still going to carry that ball around with you?" Landon teased.

"For a while," Alex said with a twinkle in his eye.

He headed to the seat next to his mother and Landon took the aisle seat.

For the first time in his life, Alex had both of his parents with him at a baseball game. The firm plastic seat had never felt more comfortable. He glanced to his left, then his right, and closed his eyes for a few seconds to savor the moment.

Marilyn thumbed the program, looking at the advertisements. "When do they start playing?" she asked.

"Right after the National Anthem."

When the National Anthem was over, Landon and Alex cheered as the Reds took the field. Marilyn pulled an emery board out of her purse and worked on her nails.

"Who's pitching today?" Landon asked.

Alex stuffed his mouth with a handful of salty popcorn.

"Gary Nolan."

"Who's pitching for the Cardinals?"

"McGlothen," Alex replied. "His ERA is 3.84; Nolan's is 2.84. Nolan should get the win, and the Reds should crush the Cardinals."

"We'll have to see," Landon replied.

Marilyn stared at them as if they were speaking a foreign language. "What are you two saying?"

Landon took a drink of his beer and started to say something, but Alex interrupted him. "I got this, Dad." He took the program from his mother's lap and opened it to the rosters. He pointed to Gary Nolan's ERA statistic. "An ERA in baseball is a pitcher's earned run average. There's a formula for calculating this stat, but I'll skip the boring details for you."

"Thank you," Marilyn said with a hint of sarcasm. "Keep it simple."

"You're feigning interest because I'm your son."

"Just keep explaining."

"Every time a runner scores, it usually counts against the pitcher's average," Alex explained. "There are exceptions, but I won't bore you with them."

Marilyn nodded slowly. "You're saying the higher the ERA, the crappier the pitcher?"

Alex shook his head. "Not always, but you get the idea."

Marilyn reached around Alex and tugged on Landon's shirtsleeve. "Does he do this for you? Explain things?"

"All the time," Landon said, smiling. "Even when I don't want an explanation."

Still filing her nails, Marilyn announced, "We should take a vacation."

With a confused look, Landon nodded slowly.

"I'm serious. We should go," said Marilyn. "As a family."

"I know where I'd like to go," Alex chimed in.

"Where?" Landon asked.

"Falmouth, Massachusetts."

Marilyn stopped filing and looked at Alex. "Why on Earth would you want to go there?"

"The Cape Cod League in Massachusetts. The Falmouth Commodores have won more championships than any other team in the last eight years."

"Do tell, what is the Cape Cod League?" Landon asked.

"It's a wooden bat league for the best collegiate players in baseball. All the major league teams scout there." Alex stuffed another handful of popcorn in his mouth.

"After the surgery," Landon said. "As soon as Uncle Bob clears you, we'll go."

Alex turned to his mom. "Were you serious? Can it be just the three of us?"

Marilyn squeezed his hand. "Yes. It can be just the three of us."

A bat cracked, and Alex and Landon were on their feet.

"What a hit!" Landon exclaimed.

"Rose is going for two," Alex yelled.

Riverfront Stadium erupted in cheers as Pete Rose stood on second base. The Myers stayed on their feet with the rest of the crowd. Dave Concepcion singled, advancing Rose to third. When the Cardinals' catcher missed a pitch to Johnny Bench, Rose stole home. Alex screamed and high-fived his mom and dad. The inning concluded on a George Foster fly ball to centerfield, and the Myers sat down.

Several moments passed before Alex spoke. "That was some serious stuff today."

Landon clapped as the Reds took the field. Marilyn was filing so fast, as if she were sanding a piece of wood. She stopped filing and reached over for Alex's hand. She squeezed it hard then went back to filing.

"You guys barely said anything in the car," Alex said.

"I had a good cry in the ladies' room," Marilyn replied.

Landon stretched upward and shifted in his seat. "How do you feel, son?"

"I'm scared, but aside from a dull headache, I feel fine."

Marilyn took two gulps of beer and set the cup under her seat. "When your dad first got into pediatric oncology," she said, "he talked a lot about his cases. He kept patient and family names confidential, of course, but he needed to talk to someone. I eventually had my fill, and for a long time I couldn't be someone to lean on. We both knew this kind of medicine would drive us crazy if we didn't find some way to deal with the heartache of watching these kids and their parents suffer. So our priest gave us all these books on suffering, which I read. Your dad leaned on a colleague who's a psychiatrist. Right or wrong, we both sort of learned how to bury our feelings."

Marilyn looked at Landon as if to toss him the conversation, and he caught it like an outfielder underneath a foul ball.

He put a hand on Alex's knee. "I compartmentalize everything about my job," he said. "Sadness is relegated to one part of my mind, doctoring in another. Emotional support stays in the middle, where I can get to it quickly for my patients and their families. When things get tough, I talk to a professional. Over the years, I've learned how to cope." He reached underneath his seat for his beer and took a drink.

"I'm not sure when all this is going to hit me, but I know it will," Alex said. "So before you two shut your emotions off, you might want to save something for me."

Landon patted Alex's knee and kept his moist eyes on the field.

Marilyn turned, draped both arms around Alex, and gave him a hug.

CHAPTER 17

DOGWOOD PARK

Friday, June 13, 1975; 5:29 a.m.

One of Landon's greatest blessings was that his sixty-five-year-old mother rose early every morning. Friday coffee was a weekly tradition that had begun in the months following his father's death. By 5:30 a.m., Landon would be through the front door and settled at the kitchen table with his mother. They sipped on mugs of black Folgers coffee, discussing the week's events and the musings of their everyday lives. By 6:50 a.m., hugs and kisses were exchanged, leaving Landon the forty minutes he needed to get from the quaint suburb of Mariemont to Children's Hospital.

Evelyn Myers's appearance defied time and space. She looked like she was in her forties. Her long blond hair had begun to turn white when she was sixty, but she still possessed a shine that turned heads. Her eyes were cobalt blue, and anyone having a conversation with her was drawn in by her gaze. She believed in wearing sunscreen long before medical experts advised consumers to do so. Her light complexion, high cheekbones, and clear skin faded any lines carved out by the sandstorms of time. At five-foot-nine, she was taller than many women her age, and her physique rivaled many of the thirty-somethings with whom she played tennis. Beyond the beautiful surface, a charming intellect, tender heart, and gentle spirit lay within her. Landon's father used to say, "God broke the mold after he made your mother. He knew he wouldn't get that close to perfection again."

She stood in front of the coffeepot in her white tennis outfit, stirring in half-and-half. Landon sat at the white laminate-topped kitchen table with white padded chairs on brushed nickel frames. He looked out the open window that faced Dogwood Park. Large walnut and sycamore trees cast westerly shadows from the morning sun. The air was still and peaceful.

Evelyn took both mugs of coffee to the table and set them down. "If you're hungry, I have a coffee cake from Graeter's."

"That sounds delicious," Landon replied. "Can't say dad would've approved."

His mother took out a plastic container from the pantry and set it on the table. She then walked to the cupboard and took out two small plates. She grabbed two forks and a butter knife from a drawer and sat down.

"I doubt your father would approve of my diet these past two years. It's not any fun cooking for one. I eat out all the time now."

"I miss him," Landon remarked. "I wish he was here."

"Me too." Evelyn took in a deep breath and let it out. "When I get sad, I think about the irony of losing him to a heart attack. He would have found the humor in that."

Landon blew over the top of his mug and took a small sip. "If you think that's ironic, wait till you hear the news I have to share."

As he relayed the events that had transpired over the past week, his mother reached out to hold his hand. The dam Landon had built to hold back his emotions finally burst and the flash flood that ensued drowned any remaining stoicism. He leaned over the table, rested his head on his arms, and sobbed. Evelyn stood up and moved her chair next to his so she could wrap him in a hug.

Landon sat up and leaned into his mom as she held him tighter. More minutes passed, and Evelyn sat there patiently until the last tear fell. Landon reached over and took several napkins out of the holder. He wiped the mucus off his upper lip, blew his nose several times, and wiped away the trails left by his teardrops. Evelyn reached down for his hand and held it tightly.

"I don't know what to do," Landon whispered. "I feel paralyzed. The thought of losing more visits and at the same time knowing I'm going to lose Alex is overwhelming."

Evelyn moved her chair back to the other side of the table. She picked up the knife and sliced the coffee cake into pieces. She scooped a big slice onto her fork, put it on a plate, and set it in front of Landon.

"You said Marilyn went with you and Alex to the game."

Landon took a bite and nodded.

"Did Jeff give any indication of what the judge might do?"

"No."

Evelyn sipped her coffee and set it down. She picked up her fork and began to cut her coffee cake into small pieces. "Marilyn might be a lot of things, but she's not cruel." Landon kept eating. "I know you don't feel that way now. But as a mom, I can tell you she's going to want Alex to spend time with his father. She might even want the three of you to spend *more* time together."

"I don't know," mumbled Landon. "She did mention the three of us taking a vacation, but I can't see Michael signing off on that."

"There *is* a difference between hatred and resentment," Evelyn replied. "Your grandma used to say, 'Hatred's a fast boil, but resentment's a slow bake.' It's taken years for Marilyn to build up her feelings toward you. She still feels hurt by you, Landon, but she doesn't hate you."

Landon spoke as he chewed. "Doesn't feel that way right now, Mom."

Evelyn mashed the coffee cake crumbs into her fork and took one last bite. "Need I remind you to leave a little room for the Lord to transform some good out of all this?"

Landon pushed his crumb-laden plate to the middle of the table. "I'd rather talk to Dad than God."

Evelyn decided not to push any further. "Talk to whoever you want, Landon. Just promise me you'll keep talking. Don't hold all this in and don't walk it by yourself."

Landon looked out the window and let his gaze fall upon a red cardinal on a boxwood bush in his mother's landscaping.

"I can keep it clinical with Alex. I can switch in and out of dad mode. I can even balance my patient load with everything I'm facing. I just can't wrap my mind around what Marilyn's trying to do to me."

"You stay focused on Alex and let the pieces fall wherever they will," Evelyn said. "He needs his father, and even more, he needs a good doctor. You can be both to him, and that's a blessing. Don't make this about Marilyn. Make it about Alex."

Landon leaned back in his chair.

"You should take your sabbatical now," said Evelyn.

"I haven't had time."

"Maybe now's the time. It's the beginning of the summer. You never know, Alex might beg his mother to spend more time with you, regardless of what happens."

Landon let out a long sigh. "I'd be shocked if she let that happen."

"You never know," Evelyn replied.

"Thanks for listening, Mom."

"It's what mothers do."

Landon got up from the table, pushed in his chair, and gave her a big hug.

"Do you have Alex this weekend?" she asked.

"I'm supposed to."

"Why don't you two come over for Sunday dinner?"

"That's a great idea."

Evelyn leaned over and gave her son a long kiss on the cheek.

Chapter 18

Sheer Bliss

Monday, June 16, 1975; 7:19 a.m.

Alex stood in front of a mirror admiring his new hospital gown. "You sexy beast," he exclaimed. "This puke green hospital gown is a gas." He sucked in his stomach and flexed his biceps. "Working the green machine. All in the front and none in the back. Oh, yeah."

Marilyn scratched her forehead. "Your mother is standing right here."

Alex whipped around in a circle and flexed again. "Let the shave queen begin."

Marilyn plugged the shaver in and turned it on while Alex sat down on the hospital bed. He pushed the button that lifted the electric bed into the sitting mode. When his mom reached over to put the shaver to his hair, Alex pushed the button that lowered the bed. He laughed as the bed lay flat, then tapped it to raise the bed again.

"You're a pain," Marilyn sneered. "Come on. We need to get this done before your dad and Uncle Bob get here."

"Just wait a second," Alex replied. "Let me run my fingers through it one more time."

Alex pushed out his lips like Mick Jagger and ran his hands through his hair like a rock star.

"You look more like a blond David Cassidy than Mick Jagger," Marilyn teased.

Alex shrugged. "My ladies like it."

"But does Emma like it?"

Alex's upturned grin fell into a frown. "That was so uncool."

Marilyn smirked. "You're the one who insisted *your* ladies like it. I was just trying to determine which one."

When she slid the shaver into the "on" position, it made a loud buzzing noise. The cool vibrating shears pinched Alex's scalp at first, but he sat still and watched as his blond hair fell like snow around him. Nurse Cindy came into the room and smiled at them both.

"Good morning," said Cindy. "Looks like things are going well."

Alex looked at all the hair in the bed. "I guess if you're a barber. Tell me this will get cleaned up before I have to sleep in it."

Cindy chuckled. "We'll transfer you to another bed, Alex."

There was a knock on the door, and Uncle Bob and Landon entered the room. Both wore scrubs. They high-fived Alex and found places to stand in the cramped hospital room.

Cindy walked over to Marilyn and spoke in a low voice.

"I'm going to get some shaving cream, a razor, and hot water. We'll need to get most of the stubble off."

Marilyn nodded. "Thank you."

"Well, sport," Bob said, "did you bring your baseball with you this time?"

Alex reached under the sheets and handed him the baseball.

"Holy cow! Bob exclaimed. "You got an autograph!"

"Joe Morgan's," Alex replied.

"You caught a foul ball off Joe Morgan, and then you got him to sign it?" Bob asked. Alex nodded. "My sons would be so jealous. That is way cool, dude. Man, if that ball could talk."

Landon smirked. "If that baseball could talk, Alex, what *would* it say?"

Alex let an ornery grin crawl across his face. "Don't hold me under sheets if you're going to fart."

The three of them belly laughed. Marilyn groaned.

"Even now, you can't talk about anything other than your farts?"

Alex shrugged.

"All right, we should carry on," Bob said, smiling. "Alex, do you want to know what we're going to do today?"

"Sure. Give me all the gory details."

Bob nodded toward Marilyn. "For your mother's sake, we're going to keep this less gory. When Nurse Cindy is done prepping your scalp, we'll take you to pre-op, where they'll hook up your IV. Dr. McIntyre, the anesthesiologist you met for your angiogram, will put you to sleep." Bob turned to Marilyn. "Landon will be scrubbing in and will be there for the whole surgery. I'd like to invite you to be with Alex during pre-op and while we're putting him under."

"I would like that, Bob. Thank you."

Bob pursed his lips and gave her a quick nod.

"Uncle Bob," said Alex, "can you tell me what you'll be doing in surgery?"

"When Nurse Cindy and your mom finish shaving your head, the nurse will mark where I need to make my incisions and cut through your skull."

"How will you actually get to my brain?" Alex asked.

"We'll make a series of punctures through the skull then cut through the bone using a special tool. We'll create what's called a skull flap. Removing the skull exposes the dura. The dura is like a piece of Saran Wrap but thicker. We'll cut that into four triangular shapes and pull the dura back to reveal the brain. Now comes the hard part—finding the tumor. I have an idea where it is, based on the angiogram. I'll make an incision near the area and look for it."

"Bob usually finds it on the first try," interrupted Landon. "He's like a metal detector for tumors."

Bob smiled. "When I find the tumor," he continued, "I'll use a tiny knife-like tool to cut out all the cancerous cells around the tumor, and then the tumor itself. Remember, we call this type of tumor an astrocytoma. Think of it as an octopus with tentacles. The tentacles sort of spread out in a star shape, and the main tumor is the octopus head. When I'm in there, I'll use tiny pliers to remove all the tentacles and the head. If I can get to it, we can get most of it. Hopefully, we can remove enough of the tumor to alleviate your symptoms and buy you some more time."

"I would prefer to be here long enough to see the Reds win the World Series," Alex said. "I think this is their year."

Bob grinned. "You're probably right."

"One more question."

"Yes?"

"How will you put my head back together?"

"We'll close up the dura," Bob said, "put a silvery mesh over the spot we exposed in your brain, and then we'll put a thin piece of rubbery goo on top of it to help everything heal. We'll put the bone piece we took out of your head back in your skull and use little metal strips with tiny screws to hold it in place until your brain and skull repair everything. It eventually will heal, Alex. And your hair will grow back."

Alex nodded. "I have one more question."

"I'm all ears," Bob replied.

"When I go under, what could go wrong?"

Alex watched his father shift his weight from one leg to another and cross his arms. Bob looked at Landon and then Marilyn.

"You should tell him," said Marilyn.

"I'm going to have to explore a bit to locate the tumor," Bob began. "There are safe and unsafe ways to do this. Sometimes I don't know the best way until I get in there or until it's too late. While I'm trying to cut out the tumor, I could cut something that affects your speech or mobility. I could accidentally brush a vein or artery while I'm trying to find the tumor, and you could bleed. Your body might not tolerate the anesthesia, and you could have a heart attack or stroke. There's a lot that could go wrong, Alex. But there's a better chance that a lot could go right."

"It's okay, Uncle Bob," Alex said matter-of-factly. "I just wanted to know the truth."

Bob put an arm around him. "You're a brave young man."

"You're a great doctor. Now I have something I want to say to you and Dad."

Marilyn walked over to the bedside. Landon leaned in to listen.

"Whatever happens today, Uncle Bob," said Alex, "I want you to know I believe you did the best you could."

CHAPTER 19

IN STITCHES

Tuesday, June 17, 1975; 9:41 a.m.

Landon finished checking on his patients then headed to Alex's hospital room. Cindy was there, wearing her white nurse's uniform and clutching a clipboard. She walked quickly toward him. He slowed his pace and braced himself for bad news. She walked past the door to Alex's room and stopped.

When Landon reached her, he asked, "What's wrong? Is it Alex?"

"Alex is fine," Cindy replied. "He's awake. I think he had some apple sauce this morning. He's doing remarkably well."

"Bob worked wonders yesterday," said Landon. "Did he come by this morning?"

"Yes."

Landon reached for the doorknob, but Cindy reached out her hand to stop him. "Your ex-wife is with Alex," she whispered.

"That's all right," said Landon. "She told me she might stop by today."

Cindy pulled the clipboard closer to her chest and leaned over to whisper. "Her husband is with her."

Landon clenched his jaw. "How long have they been in there?"

"About thirty minutes," said Cindy.

"Why are you here?" Landon asked.

She looked into Landon's eyes. "I saw them go into the room. I thought you might like someone else with you while you checked on Alex. You know, moral support. I'm supposed to take off the bandages and clean the area around the stitches this afternoon. I could do that now, and that would give you some extra time in the room without having to be alone with all of them."

Landon wanted to reach out and pull her into him, to hug her as if to say, *How can you be so beautiful and thoughtful at the same time?* Instead, he smiled and said, "Thank you." He opened the door and motioned for Cindy to walk in first. She greeted Alex with a smile.

"How are you doing?" she asked.

The blinds were drawn, and a single table lamp with a weak bulb provided light. Marilyn sat on the hospital bed on Alex's left side, holding his hand. She was dressed in white capri pants and a light-blue top. Michael stood behind her in a black suit with his hands in his pockets, looking sick to his stomach. The left side of Alex's face was black, blue, purple, and yellow-green from bruising. His left eye was swollen shut, with similar colors surrounding his eye, forehead, and temple. Yellow-green splotches, which looked like half-healed bruises, appeared along his cheekbone and down his jaw.

"Hey, sport," Landon said. "How are you feeling?"

"My face hurts, and I have a dull headache," Alex mumbled. "My face feels like it's the size of a trash-can lid."

"Well, it's not," Landon assured him. "You had your skull opened yesterday, and you're experiencing facial trauma from the surgery. This is normal, son."

"Did Uncle Bob get all of the tumor?" Alex asked.

"All of it," Landon assured him. "It was deeper than he thought, but he got it all. He put the largest chunk of it in a specimen tube with some preservative so you can see it."

"That'll be cool," Alex murmured. He closed his eyes for a few seconds then opened them again. "Was it cancer?"

Landon nodded. "Yes. A glioblastoma multiforme. You'll hear Uncle Bob and I shorten it to 'glio.'"

"Sweetie," Marilyn interrupted. "Nurse Cindy's here to change your bandages."

Alex closed his eyes for several seconds and opened them. "Okay. But I want to watch her do it."

Michael came up and put a hand on Marilyn's shoulder. "I need to head back to the office."

Marilyn nodded politely. After Michael left the room, she said, "He doesn't handle this kind of stuff well. He faints at the sight of his own blood."

"He stayed for a remarkably long time for someone who struggles in medical situations," said Cindy. "He obviously wanted to be here for you and Alex."

"He was greener than Kermit the Frog," Landon retorted.

The adults heard Alex attempt a chuckle then groan. Marilyn refrained from rushing to her new husband's defense. The corners of her mouth tightened slowly, revealing a smirk.

Cindy walked past Landon to Alex's right side. "We're

going to change your bandage and reapply an antibiotic gel to your stitching. Do you think you have the energy for that?"

Alex nodded. "Can I have some ice chips?"

"Let's raise you up first."

Cindy pressed the hospital bed button until he was sitting up, then organized supplies on the hospital tray while Marilyn spoon-fed ice chips to Alex. Landon watched as his ex-wife and Cindy worked together to care for Alex. Together they made a great team. He wondered what would happen if he and Cindy started dating. Would Marilyn accept him having another woman in his life? For a moment, the situation seemed uniquely fit for its purpose, and Landon embraced the idea that the two of them might have Alex as their common bond.

"All finished?" asked Cindy.

"Yes," Alex said with a mouthful of ice chips. He swallowed. "There's a handheld mirror in my overnight bag. Mom brought it in yesterday so I could see what I look like after the surgery. If it's okay, I'd like to watch what you're doing."

"Why don't you have your mom hold the mirror?" Cindy suggested. "I only say that because you'll be surprised at how tired you are."

Marilyn dug the mirror out of the overnight bag and waited for Cindy to finish organizing the hospital tray with supplies.

"I'll be on Alex's left side," Cindy explained. "Marilyn, why don't you sit on the bed to his right?"

Marilyn sat on the bed and held up the mirror for Alex.

"You still have your baseball, sport?" Landon asked.

Alex held up the ball, which was wrapped in a plastic bag. He spoke as the bandages were unwound from his head.

"Went with me through the whole surgery. I woke up in recovery with it in my hand."

The last of the bandages were removed. Alex shifted to sit up and tucked the baseball by his right leg. He took the mirror from his mother, turned his head to the right, and stared at a curved row of stitches along the left side of his scalp. He then looked past the mirror and noticed the adults trying to gauge his emotions.

"The stitching makes my head look like a baseball," said Alex.

Landon stood at the end of the bed. "I hadn't thought of it that way, but you're right."

Alex moved the mirror around to look at his head. "It definitely doesn't look like a Major League Baseball."

"We could open the other side of your skull. That would make it more symmetrical," Landon joked.

"Oh, no," Marilyn replied. "We're not going through that again."

"I'm not talking about the ball itself—I'm talking about the stitching," Alex said. "Please open the plastic wrap and take out my ball. There's something I want to show you."

Marilyn took the baseball from her son's hand and gave it to Landon. He removed the ball from the bag and held it up for Alex to see.

"There are three types of baseball stitching," Alex said. "The stitching on my baseball lies almost flat to the leather surface. It's called raised-seam stitching, and it's the Major League Baseball standard. Little League teams use the same size baseball, but the stitching is higher so the kid pitchers can get a better grip on the ball. It's called rolled stitching. The stitching in my head matches a flat-stitched baseball, where the stitching is so flat that it's below the leather. Teams use these types of balls for pitching machines."

Marilyn shook her head. "How do you know all this stuff?"

Alex ignored her and pointed to the baseball in his dad's hand. "The stitching on that baseball looks higher than the stitching on my head."

"What are you saying?" Marilyn asked.

"He's saying that you could use his head for batting practice," Landon replied.

Chuckles filled the hospital room.

"That's what my head feels like now," Alex replied. "Like someone's using it for batting practice."

As Cindy wrapped the last of the thick gauze around Alex's head, he noticed his mom staring at something.

"What are you looking at?" Alex asked.

"Your heart monitor," Marilyn said. "On a scale of one to ten, how bad does your head hurt?"

"Probably a six, but I feel like there's this weird pressure coming from all angles."

Landon slipped the baseball back into the plastic bag, sealed it, and placed it in his son's right hand. Alex curled his fingers around the ball, giving off a slight crinkling sound.

"I'll check with Bob to see what we can do for the pain."

When Cindy finished clearing away the old bandages, she wiped the hospital tray with disinfectant.

"I'll get you some more ice chips," she replied. "Your mom can stay a while longer, but she'll need to leave soon so you can get some rest."

Before Cindy finished her sentence, Alex had tilted his head to the right and fallen into a deep sleep.

Chapter 20
Ninth Inning

Wednesday, June 18, 1975; 4:31 p.m.

Landon finished his rounds early and went upstairs to see Alex. Bob, Cindy, and the rest of the pediatric oncology staff all commented on his son's remarkable recovery. Despite the positive news surrounding Alex, Landon's thoughts were occupied by his upcoming legal battle. Cindy had summoned him to the floor, saying Marilyn had requested he come up to see her and Alex. The note left Landon scratching his head and wondering what Marilyn had up her sleeve, particularly at a time when the two of them should be concentrating on their son instead of their "irreconcilable" differences. As he rounded the corner to go up the stairs, he spotted a slim man in a suit, with dark hair and glasses, coming down. He recognized him as Dennis Caldwell.

"Hello, Dr. Myers."

"Mr. Caldwell, what a pleasant surprise. You know, there are elevators in this hospital."

"I like the exercise," he replied. "And please call me Dennis."

"Fair enough. You can call me Landon. I suspect you're here to see Ronald."

"I stopped in on my way home from work," Dennis replied. "He still seems to be doing well."

"Minus his hair, I'm afraid," Landon replied. "He's beginning to lose it."

"His hair is the least of my worries. I just hope he can tolerate the next round of treatment."

"I'm so impressed with how well he's getting along," Landon replied. "I have to be honest—for as small as he is, I was afraid the treatments might be too much for him."

Dennis smiled. "He has his mother's spirit. Believe me, I've experienced my share of battles with him."

Landon grinned but didn't reply.

"My son met your son, Alex, in recovery last week," Dennis continued. "We've heard some whispers from the nurses that his condition is serious."

"Brain cancer," Landon replied. "It's terminal."

The worry in Dennis's taut face deepened the lines in his cheeks. "I'm sorry, Landon."

"Alex went in for surgery yesterday and seems to be recovering well. I'm hoping we've bought ourselves some more time with him."

Dennis nodded and nervously stroked his chin. He spoke in a quieter voice. "Because of you, Ronald has a chance to get better. As his father, I feel indebted to you for everything you've done to help him and my family. I'm truly sorry about Alex."

Landon suddenly felt vulnerable from the common bond he shared with Dennis. "Thank you," he replied.

The two men exchanged handshakes, and Landon climbed

a flight of stairs to the hospital floor. He walked down the hall, wiped his moist eyes, and paused in front of Alex's door. He saw Cindy hurrying down the hall. When she drew close, she pulled a tissue from her pocket and handed it to Landon.

"Your wife is in there with Alex. She has a big brown envelope in her hand."

Landon's sadness shifted to resignation. "It's probably the custody papers. I don't need my son's final weeks stained by all this crap."

Cindy reached up, lay her hand on Landon's cheek, and looked into his eyes. "Alex needs you now. You need to be strong for him."

Landon pressed his head ever so slightly into the softness of her hand. He closed his eyes for several seconds and opened them to see her shining eyes and soft face. The corners of his mouth twitched into a half smile; he lifted his hand to put it on hers. For a second, Landon wondered if this is how his father had felt about his mother.

"Thank you, Cindy," he replied.

"Nurse Cindy," she said, smiling. "Now go. Be there for *him*."

Landon walked into the room and saw Marilyn in her usual place at Alex's bedside.

"Hey, Dad," Alex said in a whisper. He stirred and closed his eyes.

Landon turned to Marilyn. "I got a note that you wanted me to come up."

She placed her hand on Alex's shoulder. "He's been sleepier today," she said.

"That's normal," Landon replied.

"I'm worried," she said softly.

"I'll be fine," mumbled Alex. He pulled his right hand from under the sheet and held up the baseball for his dad to see. "The nurses are finally letting me hold the real thing."

Landon walked over and put a hand on top of his son's. He took the other and put it underneath the baseball. Between both of his hands lay the velvety warmth of Alex's hand and the cold leather of the baseball. The rough stitching brushed against Landon's palm as he gazed at his son's discolored face.

Alex spoke with his mouth mostly closed. "Mom has something she wants to give you."

Landon tightened his hands around Alex's and looked at Marilyn. She sniffled and laid a brown envelope on the bed.

"I'm sorry," she said between sniffles. "I'm sorry for everything."

Landon softly placed Alex's hand on the bed and reached for the envelope. "What's in here?" he asked.

Marilyn wiped at her eyes. "Open it."

Landon opened the envelope and pulled out several sheets. Inside were the original custodial papers, the letter his attorney had received a week earlier, and a notarized letter from the court.

"Read the top sheet," Alex said.

The brief paragraph was only four lines. Landon focused on the second sentence with two words printed in bold that spelled out "joint custody."

Landon looked up at Marilyn with wide eyes and his mouth slightly open.

Marilyn got up from the bed, walked around to where Landon stood, and wrapped her arms around him. For a moment, Landon was thrown back in time. A time where the smell of Marilyn's honeysuckle hair and lilac perfume had made him tingle. A time when Sunday picnics and long walks along Sawyer Point were part of the family routine. A time when her gentle hugs and open arms had given him the courage and strength to become a physician.

He held her close and time stood still.

Alex struggled to open his eyes. Through the narrow slits, he saw the shadows of his parents in their embrace. Something inside him relaxed. He felt happy and at peace. He did his best to keep his eyes open for them so that they could see the joy that washed over his face. Then he heard the voices. Loud voices that increased in number. He heard them from men and women. Indistinguishable. Unrecognizable. A muffled fury of garble. Alex decided to sit up to let them know he was all right, but first, he needed to open his eyes. But he discovered he no longer had the strength to open them.

The voices, which now sounded like hundreds, suddenly vanished, and his entire body felt warm. It began at his toes and slowly crept up to his knees, thighs, and hips. The warmth oozed through his stomach and torso, past his chest, until it reached his shoulders, spilling over until it spread to his arms and wrists. It pulsed through him, like slow drips of water, until it reached his fingertips. When Alex felt the warming sensation invade his hands, he slowly opened them, and the baseball fell to the floor.

Chapter 21
Leather Memories

Saturday, June 13, 2015; 2:19pm

Lucy wiped the tears from her eyes.

"It's a sad story, sweetheart," her grandmother said.

"But a happy one, too," Lucy said through a stuffy nose. "Who were the voices?"

"The voices?" Landon asked.

"The voices at the end of the story," Lucy asked. "Were they angels?"

Landon shook his head. "No. It's how I imagined Alex hearing all the doctors and nurses after he coded."

"How did he die?" Lucy asked.

"After Marilyn and I hugged, we walked over to the bed and found him unconscious. I checked his vitals. His heart and breathing had stopped."

Lucy looked at Cindy. "Were you there, Grandma?"

Cindy nodded and took a sip of tea. "As was Uncle Bob and a small army of our colleagues."

"We think he had a brain aneurysm," Landon added. "Aneurysms were relatively common complications after brain surgery. At that time, we didn't have all the cameras and imaging systems like we do today that help guide the doctor's hands. If the surgical instruments so much as nick an artery or vein inside the brain, it weakens the vessel walls and the patient dies from a brain bleed. I was scrubbed in and standing next to Bob, watching the surgery. His hands were steady in finding and cutting out the tumor, and he took all the necessary precautions. The tumor was a tad bigger than one of those little bouncy balls. In those days, the larger the tumor, the greater the risk of brain bleeds. When Bob and I saw the size of the tumor, we knew Alex had a slim chance at a recovery without complications."

By now, Lucy's tears had dried, and her voice was stronger. "Grandpa, the other boy in the story… Did he live?"

"Ronald Caldwell," Landon confirmed. "He was the perfect patient. Strong kid. Good parents. He tolerated the treatment protocol better than any patient up to then. He was cured and is still living. I think he's somewhere out west."

"Denver," said Cindy. "He invited your grandfather to his high school graduation."

"A lot of my patients invited me to milestones like that," Landon said. "I went to as many as I could so that I could celebrate their lives with them. I was always in a partnership with my patient, like two soldiers trapped in a foxhole during a bombardment. In some ways, we relied on each other to survive."

"But you had the medicine," Lucy replied.

"Yes, and they had to have the will to live," said Landon.

Lucy pulled one more Oreo from the package and took a

bite. She crunched on the cookie as she spoke. "Did you ever see Marilyn again?"

"Oh, yes," Landon replied. "We stayed in contact for a while."

"She went to the Reds' pennant game with us that fall," Cindy added.

"And the World Series," said Landon. "Alex was right. The Reds won big that year."

"Is Marilyn still in Cincinnati?" Lucy asked.

Landon sighed. "We lost her a year after Alex passed. She was heading east on Columbia Parkway. Some clown was driving drunk on the wrong side of the highway and hit her car head-on. She died at the scene. Michael was inconsolable. It was a very sad funeral."

"Do you still keep in touch with him, Grandpa?"

"No. Michael moved to Hilton Head shortly after the accident. After the funeral, we never saw him again."

Lucy took another bite of her Oreo. "So let me get this straight. Everybody in your life, at that time in your life, is gone now?"

"Some of my doctor friends are still around. But yes, nearly everyone I had at that time disappeared in a matter of twelve to fourteen months. Your great-grandma was still active then, playing tennis and volunteering. Marilyn's funeral was particularly hard on her. They'd always been close. She was like a daughter to her."

"I always wondered if it was your mother who got Marilyn to agree to joint custody," said Cindy. "I'll bet she called her after that Friday visit."

Landon shrugged. "Maybe."

Lucy took the last bite of her cookie and looked down at her phone. "Dad's going to be here any minute."

"Any more questions?" Landon asked.

"A couple," Lucy replied. "It's June thirteenth. Alex died on June eighteenth."

Landon nodded. "That's right."

"Do you and Grandma do anything special on that day?"

"If the Reds are in town, we go to the game," said Cindy. "If not, we go to the cemetery. Just the two of us. We don't make a big deal about it."

"Some years we don't do either," Landon added.

"One more question. When did you and Grandma start to date?"

Landon smiled. "I started dating her about a month after Alex's funeral."

"We ate in the cafeteria a lot," Cindy said with a gleam in her eye. "I didn't think he was ever going to ask me out."

"Where did he take you on your first date?" Lucy asked.

"Where do you think?" Cindy replied.

Lucy shrugged and shook her head. "I don't know, dinner and a movie?"

Cindy laughed. "Sweetie, your grandpa took me to a baseball game."

Lucy groaned. "You guys sure love baseball. This whole family is obsessed with it."

"Your Uncle Alex was obsessed with it," said Landon. "You have him to thank for that."

The response startled Lucy for a moment. Cindy put an arm around her shoulders. "That's right," she said. "Alex would've been your uncle."

The three of them heard a car pull into the driveway.

"That must be Danny," Cindy said.

Landon stared at his granddaughter's soft fingers clutching Alex's baseball.

"I was startled when you found that," he mumbled. "You know, Lucy, the last sixteen-year-old to hold that ball was your dad."

She heard her father's footsteps in the living room, and when he came into the kitchen, he looked down at the table and smiled.

"Well, what do you have there?"

Lucy looked down at the worn leather and faded stitching, then up at her grandpa. "The baseball."

ACKNOWLEDGMENTS

I want to offer my humble gratitude to some special people:

To my daughters, Samantha and Grace, who fell in love with this old book idea and persistently pestered me to complete it; to my wife Kristine, who said, "I love you. Listen to your kids."

To Marvin Lopez, MD; Fred Theye, PhD; and Rick Bauer, CRNA, for assisting me with my medical research.

To my editors, Steve Parolini and Angela Brown, for their friendship, counsel, and skill.

To Garrick Bauer, James "Buz" Ecker, Patti Normile, and Ryan Webster, for helping me work through plot and character ideas, editing first drafts, and providing a safe sounding board.

To family and friends who continue to support me by reading drafts and offering feedback.

About the Author

James Flerlage is the author of *Before Bethlehem,* a critically acclaimed historical novel and "2013 Recommended Book" by *Kirkus Reviews.*

In addition to spending time with his family, James enjoys fishing, drumming, and watching Major League Baseball; he follows the Kansas City Royals and the Cincinnati Reds.

Follow James and *The Baseball*, via Instagram:
@thebaseballbook

To contact the author, please email
jamesflerlage@gmail.com